DATE DUE

Demco

LINC

MARY BLOUNT CHRISTIAN

LINC

Macmillan Publishing Company
New York

Maxwell Macmillan Canada
Toronto

Maxwell Macmillan International
New York   Oxford   Singapore   Sydney

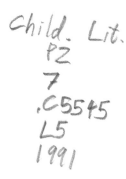

Macmillan Publishing Company is part of the Maxwell Communication
Group of Companies.

Macmillan Publishing Company
866 Third Avenue
New York, NY 10022

Maxwell Macmillan Canada, Inc.
1200 Eglinton Avenue East
Suite 200
Don Mills, Ontario M3C 3N1

First edition
Printed in the United States of America

10   9   8   7   6   5   4   3   2   1
The text of this book is set in 11 point Janson.

Library of Congress Cataloging-in-Publication Data
Christian, Mary Blount.
Linc / Mary Blount Christian. — 1st ed.
p.   cm.
Summary: Linc, a sensitive, artistic teenager, can do nothing to
please his father, a former high school football hero, until Linc
agrees to join him on a deer-hunting expedition.
ISBN 0-02-718580-X
[1. Fathers and sons—Fiction.   2. Family problems—Fiction.
3. Hunting—Fiction.]   I. Title.
PZ7.C4528Li 1991   [Fic]—dc20   91-3596

For Edie Carlton-Abbey and Laura Hsu,
who believe that learning
is a continuing process

LINC

1

LINCOLN Chandler rolled the medium-dark charcoal pencil between his nimble fingers and gazed past his sketch pad toward Ginger Rawlings. With a shell-pink muslin scarf draped loosely around her leotard, she looked like a Greek goddess as she worked out at the barre, moving on point from an *attitude* to an *arabesque*.

Grinning involuntarily, Linc made quick, light strokes across his pad almost without taking his eyes off her. Ginger made a terrific subject. Her usually pale ivory face was flushed peach from the strenuous exercises she'd been repeating for the last hour, and perspiration glistened like sparkle dust on her neck and shoulders.

Grabbing a charcoal pencil with a softer point, Linc corrected the chin. He felt he'd captured her lithe figure pretty well. It was the expression he could never quite mirror. How could he make it happen on paper?

He cocked his head and studied the sketch. Not bad. He'd caught the highlight on Ginger's taut calf muscles and her high cheekbones, which she'd exaggerated with blusher. Early on he'd learned the importance of a working knowledge of anatomy, of bone structure and muscle tone. If he didn't have that, his figures would look as if they were formed of soft putty. No, except for that elusive expression, it was not a bad likeness of Ginger at all. He felt pleased with himself, sort of.

"You're laughing," Ginger said. She was standing with her toes turned out, hands on her slender hips, staring intently at him.

Linc's grin spread across his face as his eyes darted to his pad and back to meet hers. "No, I'm not."

"Yes, you are! You're laughing at me. What's so funny? Wasn't I holding my arms correctly?"

Linc forced himself to scowl. "Is this better?" How could he tell her he was pleased with himself, pleased with his work? Self-esteem was a feeling he so rarely enjoyed that he couldn't handle it well.

Not that he shouldn't be able to make a decent sketch of Ginger. He'd sketched maybe a hundred pictures of her since they'd begun seeing each other a few weeks into the year.

Ginger had definitely gotten junior year off to a good start. He'd been admiring her as she moved gracefully through the crowds of kids in the halls. Ginger had attended the high school for performing arts in Houston until her father got tired of traffic and set up a law practice here over the summer. When Ginger had noticed Linc making a quick sketch of her in the cafeteria, she'd confronted him. Within the week he'd summoned enough courage to ask her out on a date. They'd doubled with his best friend, Dink Tobridge, and Sandra Hall, and had been "together" ever since—as much as they could be with her spending every waking hour stretching, practicing, and rehearsing.

Linc flipped through the sketch pad. There were twenty sketches of Ginger in this pad alone. Then he flipped one more page, to where he'd attempted a family portrait. His mother, with her tawny brown hair falling over her delicate shoulders, her hazel eyes wide; his sister, Betty, a young duplicate of his mother; his father, with sun-streaked sandy hair, deep-set brown eyes, and wide, short neck; and himself, a featureless blob. Why couldn't he fit himself into that portrait?

Linc laid the pad and pencils on the gym floor beside himself and flexed his cramped fingers, leaning forward to take the pressure off his tailbone. He hadn't realized how long he'd been drawing.

Why was it that he could grasp and intricately control a tiny pencil, but fail so miserably with a big football? Could he really be that adept in one area and hopeless in another? Or was his failure at sports some sort of rebellion against his ultrajock father?

Ginger had resumed her stretches at the barre. Her leotard was so sweat-moistened now that he could see the outline of her bra. Linc dropped his gaze to stare at his hands, suddenly uncomfortable with the feelings that swept over him like a boiling hot wave.

He jumped guiltily when she called to him, "Come 'ere, Linc. I need your help."

Unfolding his long legs, Linc stood hesitantly to face her, realizing that she was asking him to partner her. "I don't wanna," he said. Man, if his father could see him now, he'd go into a real tirade.

"Oh, come on," she teased as she walked over to him and held both his hands in hers, "Are you afraid someone's going to see you and think you're a sissy? I've never met anyone so man-image conscious."

Linc laughed out loud. "It's not me! It's my father. Sometimes I think he believes I'm gay just because I'm not on the football team."

Ginger giggled. "I'll vouch for you, if you want." Frowning slightly, she said, "You've got to be tough to be in ballet. It's extremely rigorous. In fact, I've heard that some professional football players take ballet to heighten their agility on the field."

"Not *my* dad, I can guarantee you."

Cocking her head to one side, Ginger focused her liquid brown eyes on his blue-green ones. "Maybe if your dad had taken some ballet, he wouldn't have been injured and ended his career so young."

Linc looked away quickly. "That's another story," he said. "Maybe someday I'll share it." Someday, when he'd come to terms with it himself.

With her fingers, Ginger turned Linc's face back toward her. "Please, Linc, help me with my practice. I promise, nobody's going to see you. Besides, what if they did?" She crooked her finger and motioned for him to follow. "Ronald can't practice today. How am I going to be a wonderful Clara in *The Nutcracker* on Christmas Eve if I don't practice my *pirouettes* and *fouettés* with a partner? Just put your hands on my waist, like this." She grabbed his hands and placed them so that his fingers were just above her hips.

His hands felt clammy. Was that her perspiration or his? Linc could feel his face growing hot, and his whole body tingled beneath the skin. Clearing his throat nervously, Linc said, "I don't see how you can do so many spins without getting dizzy."

"It's all in the snap of the head," Ginger said. "Okay, just loosely," she instructed. "Now, I'll just—"

Ginger spun in his grasp. Then suddenly she stopped, and, giggling, she put her arms around his neck and kissed him on the cheek.

Linc tensed and swallowed hard. His armpits felt damp,

and he could feel sweat beads popping out above his lips. "Somebody'll be coming soon to lock the gym," he almost whispered.

"Maybe." Ginger pressed her body to his and kissed him again, this time on the lips.

Linc could feel his heart pounding against his rib cage. He thought it might explode. Pushing her away abruptly, he said, "Don't!" His voice was sharper than he'd intended.

Ginger drew back, looking at him wide-eyed. "What's the matter? Don't you care about me? If you're worried that we might let things get out of hand, well, I told you I'm on the pill."

She looked down and away from him, and Linc saw how dark and thick her lashes were. Ginger was scaring him. She was so much more sophisticated than he was. And there were things about him that she didn't know, things he wasn't ready to share with her—or with anyone.

"It's not that I was expecting a heavy relationship, of course," she continued. "The doctor—he's been our family doctor since I was a baby—he thought I ought to, for a minor problem, that's all—but whatever the reason for taking the pill, I'd still be okay, you know? I mean, the pill's ninety-nine percent sure."

Bless Ginger and her nervous chatter. The mood was gone. Linc shifted his arms across his chest. "You can't be sure! What if *you* were part of that *one percent*? What if—"

Ginger waved clenched fists. "But I wouldn't be. Linc, you make me crazy! Talk to me, Linc. Tell me what's the matter. Is it me? You don't love me? Is it something else?" Then she stopped for a second. "Would it be your first time? Are you scared?"

"No!" Linc lied. He shook his head as if to clear it of thoughts. "I gotta go." How could he tell her the truth, that he was scared of his own feelings? And that he was afraid of their winding up like his parents, kids having kids, having to give up their ambitions in life and settle for just existing.

What could be worse than getting married so young? If Mom hadn't been pregnant, maybe she'd have finished school and gone on to college, become somebody besides a wife and mother. Maybe she'd even have married someone else. Somebody besides "Chan the Man" Chandler. Linc heaved a wistful sigh. Maybe Chan would've been an NFL coach or even a network sportscaster by now, instead of the manager of a sporting goods store in a nowhere town like Glory.

Linc couldn't do that to Ginger—not beautiful, talented Ginger. Didn't she realize how he felt, just being around her? He stroked her arms as he spoke. "Do you know how many high-school romances survive graduation? Not many last past the summer after."

"Linc, one of your most appealing traits is that you think ahead. But why do you have to settle on the absolutely worst-case scenarios? Sometimes things come out great!"

Chuckling, Linc rested his arms on her shoulders and pressed his lips to her forehead. "I guess I've always been a worrier. I'm glad you find it appealing."

Ginger would be a ballerina someday, a famous ballerina, if she didn't screw up her life with him. She had the talent and the ambition. The others in the company looked like elephants next to her. All Ginger needed was the opportunity. She talked about going away to a famous ballet school after graduation, so what place did he have in her future, anyway?

And what would *he* be? He was a nobody in school, an average student in everything except art. But what was the use of excelling in art when he was average in P.E.? What a disappointment to the great "Chan the Man."

Linc glanced at his watch. "Egad! I really *do* have to go! Dad'll be home any minute now. It's trash day, and—" He pecked Ginger on the cheek and grabbed his sketch pad and pencils. "See you tomorrow. And I do lo—care about you. See you!"

His heart thumped against his rib cage as he dashed down the gym steps and to his '68 Chevy, parked out back. He had to beat his father home. He just had to. If he didn't get the trash cans put away, Chan would be furious. His father loved to yell at him and make him feel stupid. And lately, Chan had been worse than usual.

Linc spun the car around and paid little attention to the two stop signs between the school and his house. He rounded the corner of Petrie and Lawnsford and saw a tan jeep just ahead of him. If he'd had any doubts that it was his father's jeep, the bumper stickers would have convinced him. GUNS DON'T KILL PEOPLE, PEOPLE KILL PEOPLE, and IF YOU THINK COPS ARE BAD, NEXT TIME YOU'RE IN TROUBLE CALL A HIPPIE.

The two trash cans were on their sides at the edge of the driveway. Linc pulled up in front of his house, jammed his gear into park, and left the motor running. He made a dash across the lawn toward the cans.

Linc felt a red hot rock in his throat as the jeep swerved to the right, deftly flattening one of the cans. The jerk, the lousy creep! He'd deliberately run over it! He could have missed them both, but he just couldn't resist the opportunity for another confrontation with his only son, his big disappointment in life.

A picture flashed through Linc's mind of the bike he'd gotten for his tenth birthday. He'd forgotten to put it away one evening and found it bent and irreparable the next morning. Even then he'd suspected his father had run over it. Now he was sure. The next Christmas he'd gotten a new bike, but it wasn't the same.

Clarke Chandler gunned the jeep's motor and drove into the garage, stopping with a squeal of brakes just before the bumper hit the back wall of the garage. He paused momentarily as he swung from the jeep and glanced icily at Linc before heading into the house without saying a word. His face looked pale and glassy.

Linc knew he'd have plenty to say later. His father would never miss an opportunity to tell Linc what he thought of him.

Linc put the two cans at the back of the house. He could try to hammer the bent one later, maybe make it usable again. He returned to his car and parked it properly at the curb, locking it. Taking a deep wistful breath, he headed around the house toward the rear door.

2

LINC slipped his sketch pad inside his looseleaf notebook as he pushed through the back door and into the kitchen. With red potatoes steaming on the range and fresh bread baking in the oven, the room was warm and humid.

His father, the garbage can mauler, was already hunkered over the gray Formica table, his large and powerful fingers tenderly caressing a can of Pearl beer. Without him the room, with its ruffled gingham curtains and fresh-cut carnations, might have seemed to belong to a cozy television family.

Chan looked at Polly Chandler. "Are you putting on weight, Pol? Maybe you ought to cut back on the feedbag. You know how I feel about fat women," he said before taking a lingering swig.

Linc stared at the beads of moisture on the shiny silver can, not wanting to look at his father and maybe give away his own anger. Chan was picking on his wife because he was mad at his son! And look at Chan! He was muscular, sure, but not *all* that bulk was muscle. He was developing quite a gut, himself.

Polly Lincoln Chandler was leaning over the kitchen sink, scraping carrots and making nervous chatter, the way she always did when Linc and his dad were in the same room, as if she could throw up a barrier of words that would keep peace between them.

Just once, Mom, tell him to shove it, Linc wished silently.

"Sally Strand got a new car yesterday, Stuart's Christmas present to her," she said instead. "A blue Ford, one of the compacts, with windows that roll up at the push of a button and a defroster for the back window and—"

The vein in Clarke Chandler's temple throbbed visibly. He took another swig, then put the can down with a thump. "Is that what you want, Pol? To go into debt for some fancy car to go to the grocery store in?"

"No, Chan, I didn't mean—"

"Stuart Strand has a bimbo on the side; he got *her* a BMW. It's common knowledge," Chan growled between swigs of beer. "Besides, they don't have any kids needing stuff all the time."

Linc grimaced. Leave it to his dad to turn the simplest piece of gossip into a put-down for the rest of them. Linc noticed his mother's fingers tighten on the scraper. God, but he wished she'd get back at Chan—just once. He swallowed hard. "Nice outfit, Mom," he interrupted. "New, isn't it? Did you make it? You really should've been a fashion designer, you know. You'd be famous!"

Maybe if he planted a seed, she'd realize she could be more than a mother and wife. "I see they're having some business courses in continuing education at the high school, if you're interested."

Her shoulders were arched stiffly, and she didn't turn around, but Linc could see her mist-muted reflection in the window above the sink. "I made the buttonholes too big, I think, and it doesn't hang just right." She didn't even break the rhythm of the scraping as she spoke.

"No, it's terrific," Linc insisted.

"Your father is home, Linc. Can't you say hello?"

Linc felt his face go slack and clammy as the kindly mother turned into a wicked witch right before his eyes. The aftershock of betrayal shivered through his body the way it had when he was little. Then he had loved her one minute but feared her the next as she had lost patience with the bad little boy and contorted her face in a shriek or spanked him—hard. That was before she'd learned the magic words that turned him into the "good" child. "Wait till your father gets home."

Linc cut a quick glance toward his father, who was again concentrating on his beer. "We *saw* each other outside already." He pushed past his mother and edged toward the swinging door between the kitchen and the dining room. "I—I guess I'd better get started on my homework, if you don't need me for anything. Semester finals come up next week, you know."

He let the door swing closed behind him and then hurried upstairs to his room. That was the only place in the whole house where he didn't feel that he was being judged. He flung his books onto his bed and took off his jacket, hanging it on the hook behind the door.

His father's muffled voice rose through the heating vents and curled around his head like a too-tight sweatband. " . . . quit school . . . family . . . money."

Linc flopped onto his bed and pressed his hands over his ears. He didn't have to hear the whole conversation to know what was being said. He'd heard it often enough. All about how "Chan the Man" 's brilliant football career had been sacrificed when he had to go to work and support his family, about how nobody appreciated how hard he worked, how his boss didn't give him enough money, and on and on and on. Why take it out on the rest of them? Was it their fault?

A quiet tap at the door made Linc jump. He sat up and said, "Yes?"

"It's me, Betty. Can I come in? I need to talk."

Linc's sister hurried in at his invitation and left the door slightly ajar. She picked nervously at a spot on her brown plaid slacks as she spoke. "Linc, you've got to help me. Jeffrey Ballard asked me to the Christmas ballet, and I want to go so bad. I can't tell him Dad won't let me go out on dates, and I'm afraid Jeffrey will think I don't like him, but I do! I mean, I'm probably the only almost fifteen-year-old girl at Glory who's not allowed to date yet."

Linc lay back on his bed, using his clasped hands as a pillow. "What do you think I can do about it? Tell me about this Jeffrey who's got my kid sister all hot and bothered. What makes him worth me getting my tail caught in a crack over?"

Betty's hazel eyes darkened under her scowling brows. "First of all, you've got to stop even *thinking* of me as your *kid* sister! I'm *not* a kid anymore. I'm a woman."

Linc sniggered.

She reached over and popped him on the stomach. "Girls mature faster than boys, so I'm at least your age, if not a year older, physically and mentally." Her expression was dead serious.

Maybe *that* was his problem! He was just maturing slowly, a late bloomer. This time next year he'd probably fill out with muscles and weight that would make Chan—

"Are you listening? Look at me so I'll know you're listening to me!" Betty tossed her head haughtily, and her straight, coarse hair settled once again on her shoulders.

Linc nodded gravely, sat up, and looked straight into Betty's eyes.

Obviously satisfied that she had his attention, she said, "Jeffrey's sixteen already. He got his driver's license the day he turned, and I'm the first girl he's asked out on a date where he can drive himself." Betty's pride was evident from her suddenly erect posture. "He's such a hunk, I've just got to go!"

Scowling, Linc said, "Only sixteen, huh? You sure you're not too *old* for him? I mean, you being so mature and all."

"I'm serious, Linc. If you don't help me, I'll probably die an old maid, broken and bitter and living like a bag lady on the skids in some crime-infested area of a city."

Linc grinned at his sister. Somehow he couldn't imagine anyone as vivacious and pretty as Betty winding up unmarried if she chose otherwise.

Betty was pretty—and very different from Linc. His own hair was almost chestnut and his eyes blue-green. He favored no one in the family, actually. Until he had snooped in an off-limits desk drawer when he was ten and found his birth certificate, he'd fantasized that he'd been adopted, or kidnapped from gypsies by a band of roving conservative Chandlers.

That was when he'd found his parents' marriage license, too, signed by a justice of the peace in the next county, and learned he had been born just four months into their marriage. He'd asked his friend Dink about babies, and Dink had asked his parents and relayed the information, a bit garbled in the translation, but accurate enough to make Linc realize that his parents had married because of him. He hadn't mentioned his discovery to them or to Betty, but he would never forget that it wasn't choice that had made Mom drop out of school and marry Chan. It was him.

"I know it's tough—and unfair—Betty, that they won't let you go out on dates—"

13

"*He*, Linc, *he* won't let me go out on dates. Mama would, if he would. I mean, she told me all that junk about what boys want and don't let them have it and stuff like that when I was just a kid. I think she'd let me go if *he'd* loosen up!"

Linc shook his head. "Yeah, I guess you know it all, then, but I don't know what I can do." It was the old double standard. They didn't seem to worry much about him dating, but they overprotected Betty.

"*Please*, Linc! It's important to me, really! And if you do this, you don't have to get me anything for Christmas! And I'll owe you a great big favor, too. Just ask and it's yours."

He stared at his hands, thinking. "I suppose it never hurts to have your sibling owe you one. Ginger's starring in the ballet this year, she's Clara. Maybe I could take you, and you could meet Jeffrey there."

Betty shook her head vigorously. "Jeffrey would know we were sneaking, and I'd die of embarrassment. It won't work."

"Well, what if you ask Jeffrey if I can bum a ride with you? I promise, I'll disappear the minute we get there. Then, as far as the folks are concerned, Jeffrey is giving us both a ride." Maybe, just maybe, they could pull it off. After all, their folks *were* being grossly unfair to Betty.

Betty gave Linc a quick squeeze, then hopped up. "You're terrific!"

"Save your celebration until we're back home safely," Linc said. "You do realize that we stand a chance of winding up locked in our rooms until we're thirty." Grounding had become the big punishment when their parents realized that it hurt more than the quick spankings. Once Linc had counted up the total hours spent in his room, and it had come to something like six weeks.

Betty bolted for the door. "He's worth the trouble!" She slipped out and closed the door behind her.

Linc shrugged. For her, maybe. He was probably being stupid, going out on a limb for his kid sister. But she'd never been the kind of creepy sibling who spied or tattled. And there'd been plenty of times when she could have gotten him into trouble.

He caught a glimpse of himself in the full-length mirror attached to the closet door. Making a fist, he brought his arm up to make a muscle. He felt it with his other hand. Had he developed since the last time he'd checked? He stood up and assumed a bullish pose in front of the mirror, turning a bit to the left and back again, studying his reflection.

It was no use. It wasn't that he didn't have strength; he'd done enough yard work to develop that. And in his room he'd secretly worked out on the equipment his dad had given him. Secretly, because he hated for Chan to think he'd tried and failed at muscle building or that he cared at all. But it was no use. He was destined to be wiry, and no football player.

Even as a little kid, he'd had no real interest in the game. Yet he'd struggled at it. He'd tried, reaching for that ball until his fingers ached, feeling it thud into his tender stomach again and again, until he had to run inside crying and hide.

"Linc!" his mother called from downstairs. "Supper!"

They ate in the dining room just off the kitchen, with blue linen placemats and matching napkins his mother had sewn, and silk daffodils in a vase. What an illusion of the picture-perfect, television sitcom family—the football hero, his high-school sweetheart, and their adorable children, all living in a well-kept, well-decorated home.

Wearing his gray sweats emblazoned in red with I AM

15

THE COACH, DO AS I SAY, his father seemed to be in a merry mood. Three beers tended to do that. He was already at the table, as was Linc's mother. Betty slipped in behind Linc and slid into her chair across from Polly. His sister looked apprehensive, and Linc realized that she was expecting him to do something about Jeffrey right then and there.

"Potatoes?" she asked, shoving the bowl toward Chan. He heaped several serving spoonfuls onto his plate, then passed them back to Polly. She shook her head, passing them on to Betty. Linc couldn't help noticing that there was very little on his mother's plate. Chan's remark about her weight must have hit a sensitive nerve.

Linc concentrated on spreading margarine on the still-warm bread. Mostly they ate in silence, probably because Polly was still brooding and Chan was concentrating on his plate. And neither Linc nor Betty wanted to be the first to say something that might be misinterpreted and start an argument.

Whenever he had dinner at Dink's house, he was struck by the good-humored chatter at the table, but that hardly happened at the Chandlers'. "Your father's had a hard day," his mom would caution him and Betty when they were children. "So see how quietly you can eat tonight." Chan's hard days rolled into weeks, months, and years, it seemed. It just became the habit to eat silently, or maybe it was that they had nothing to say to one another.

Linc felt a kick on his shin. He looked up to see Betty frowning.

He swallowed hard. "The annual production of *The Nutcracker* ballet is coming up Christmas Eve. Ginger has a big part in it this year." His voice sounded almost falsetto. He cleared his throat, embarrassed.

"That's nice," Mrs. Chandler said.

Linc cleared his throat, took a drink of milk, and continued under Betty's anxious eye. "Yes, this year she's playing Clara. It's a big break for her. There are usually recruiters from ballet companies in the audience. If she does well, it could mean a place in the ballet school she wants to go to after graduation." His heart suddenly felt empty at the thought of Ginger leaving Glory.

"At least you don't have to worry about your girlfriend getting it on with one of those sissy boys in tights she dances with," Chan said without looking up.

The muscles in Linc's neck tightened, but he didn't change expressions. He wouldn't give Chan the pleasure of knowing he was getting to him. "Ginger says lots of professional football players take ballet to make them more agile on the field. She says—" He stopped short of saying that it helped avoid injuries. He didn't want to make Chan remember or get angry. "I'd like to take Betty with me, if you don't mind," Linc said. "I think she'd enjoy it a lot."

"Oh!" Betty said. "That would be great, Linc! I'd love it! I'd love to see Ginger dancing Clara. Thank you so much for asking!" Betty was laying it on a little thick. Surely their folks would suspect something. He scowled at her, hoping she'd understand and shut up.

Chan still didn't look up, and Polly didn't say anything, either, for a moment. Then she spoke. "The costumes are so lovely in that ballet. And the music is so—"

"You'd be there with her?" Chan said, finally looking at Linc.

"Oh, yes," Linc promised. His chair creaked beneath him as he shifted uneasily. "Same car, same auditorium, right there." It wasn't really a lie. After all, he didn't say right next to her, did he?

"I guess it's all right then," Chan said. "But don't take her to any of those hangouts afterwards."

Linc was tempted to give in, but Betty's frantic look made him try one more time. "It starts so early, even if we stopped off for a burger afterward, we'd be home in plenty of time, and Ginger would be hurt if we didn't congratulate her. I was thinking about taking some flowers backstage. I believe that's traditional."

Linc's mother flashed her first smile of the evening. "That would be a lovely gesture, don't you think, Chan?"

"I'll keep my eye on Betty, I promise." Linc forced himself to grin. "After all, Dad, we don't have to worry about her backstage, do we?"

Chan reached over and clapped a hand on Linc's shoulder, returning the grin. Camaraderie at last, even for a moment. "Right! But you'd better be home by eleven. Your grandparents will be here for Christmas, and I don't want you two sleeping late, understood? There'll be plenty to do to help out your mom."

"Understood, Dad," Linc said, finally able to breathe again. He glanced at Betty. "Right, Betty?"

She nodded.

Pushing back his chair, Chan dropped his napkin beside his plate. "You aren't getting serious about this girl, are you, Linc?"

"Oh, gosh, no!" Linc lied. "She's just fun to be with, that's all." Fun. He shouldn't have said fun.

The vein in Chan's neck pulsated. "You aren't going steady with her?"

Linc felt warm all over. "She rehearses practically all the time. And I guess we haven't had more than six real dates since I met her in September." He shouldn't have said that, either. Chan would figure they'd been doing some heavy making out in the school parking lot. "Uh, I'll help you put stuff away, Mom. Betty's probably got some phone calls to make."

Betty blinked at him, slack jawed. "Huh? Oh, yeah!"

"Don't stay on the phone too long," Chan said.

Polly gathered up the bowls and carried them to the refrigerator. She could never tolerate clutter, not even for a moment. She always aligned magazines with the edges of the coffee table and continually plumped and rearranged throw pillows on the sofa with nervous energy.

Chan left for the den, probably to read the sports pages and watch television, or maybe to bask among the glistening gold-plated football trophies and animal heads that were jammed into every available space there. As a child, Linc imagined his own head mounted there, right between the moose and the wild boar. He still felt uncomfortable in that room, although the thought of mounting a crushed garbage can made it seem a bit more pleasing.

Betty leaned close to Linc's ear and whispered. "You didn't mention Jeffrey, Linc. What about Jeffrey?"

Linc winked at her. "One step at a time. Don't worry, okay?"

She smiled slightly, then snatched up the remaining silverware and plates. "Okay," she said, "if you say so."

Linc heard the doubt in her voice. He hurried back to his room. Why should Betty worry when he could worry enough for both of them?

3

THE week before, Linc had driven Ginger to her costume fitting, and she'd talked him into staying. Now, in his room, he incorporated every detail of the costume into a sketch on tracing paper. When he was satisfied with it, he transferred the costume onto one of the figures he'd sketched earlier.

He drew a Christmas tree to one side in the background, and on the other side he drew the nutcracker soldier dueling with a fierce-looking rat. To each side of the picture, he added stage curtains. This was fun! It reminded him of all the children's stories he'd drawn.

The drawing should make a fairly nice extra Christmas gift, to go along with the sterling barrettes he'd gotten Ginger. They had promised each other they wouldn't spend much money on their gifts.

Linc held the sketch at arm's length, studying it. Who was he kidding? The Christmas tree looked too large, and he was sure the rat's uniform was inaccurate. This sketch wasn't nice enough to give as a gift; none of his sketches were. He couldn't even draw himself, he thought, remembering the family portrait.

Maybe he wouldn't make the sketch a real gift. He'd just

hand it to Ginger at school as a memento of the night she'd danced Clara. Or maybe he'd stick it away in the back of his closet, along with the others. No big deal. After all, he'd had only the training in school, which wasn't much, plus the lessons in how-to books he'd secreted in his room.

Chan had always hated it when Linc closeted himself with art supplies. "You oughta be outside, tossing a few with the other boys," he'd say. "No wonder you look so pale and skinny. You need sunshine!" So Linc would put away his pencils and crayons and go outside. But sooner or later, most of the time, he'd come in with a gash over his eye or the wind knocked out of him and creep up to his room, resentful and humiliated.

But he wasn't a sissy. He'd handled himself fairly well the few times he'd been challenged and couldn't talk his way out of a fight. And he wasn't gay. He didn't have any trouble identifying himself sexually, not with his hormones using jackhammers whenever he was around Ginger! He just wasn't athletic. Why couldn't Chan understand that?

But if he was really good at art, why didn't his folks encourage him to learn more? There were people making good bucks—better than Chan made at the sporting goods store—drawing advertisements and designing buildings or clothes. And there were cartoonists and courtroom artists and plenty of other professionals in the field of art. It wasn't as if he would have to live in squalor.

It seemed that if Chan's son wouldn't play football on national television for megabucks, Chan didn't give a damn what he did. At least, that was Linc's impression.

"So you don't have the weight on you to be running back like me," Chan had said in Linc's freshman year. "We'll work on your throwing arm. A quarterback lives by his arm, his wits, and good guards."

21

All during his fourteenth summer, they'd worked out, with Chan driving Linc to be better than he was capable of being. Linc had broken a few neighbors' windows and a couple of bones, but he hadn't developed the strength to give the ball distance and accuracy.

"You're wiry, so maybe you'd be better on the special team, running the ball back from the kick-off, or for punting for extra points," Chan had said Linc's sophomore summer. By the end of it, Linc had tried everything but water boy. Football just wasn't in his future, and once Chan knew it, he gave up on Linc. But it obviously galled him that his son was soft in sports, and sentimental to boot.

The following fall Linc had tried every other sport known to humanity, hoping he could give his father something to brag about at the sporting goods store: soccer, basketball, baseball, even golf. But he seemed always to be falling over his own feet. Finally Chan became convinced that he had not one daughter, but two.

Betty wasn't the least bit interested in art or music. She'd tried hard to win Chan's love, too. She was on the girl's volleyball team, but Chan didn't seem to notice, not even when she won a state championship letter. She was, after all, *only* a girl. Why did they have to get stuck with a Neanderthal man for a father? Linc wondered.

Although he didn't look like his mother, Linc felt pretty sure that he'd inherited his artistic interest from her. Her own interests had taken other turns, but she was creative. She designed and made her own clothes and every bed-spread, drape, and upholstered piece in the house.

Ever since Linc had been in school, his mother had donated homemade articles for the school bazaars, and they always went for top dollar. People inevitably asked her where she had bought her contributions. Had she stayed in school, gone on to college, she could have been a fashion designer or interior decorator. Surely she could recognize talent in art. But apparently she didn't see anything good about his work. Or else she just wanted him to be a different person—to please Chan.

Linc tore the sketch from his pad. So it was lousy. He shrugged. He'd give the sketch to Ginger anyway. At least it would show her he was thinking about her, and maybe it would serve as an apology for his behavior today.

"It's beautiful!" Ginger told him the next morning at school. They were hovering against the wall, out of the wind, waiting for the first bell to ring and the big front doors to open.

"No big deal," Linc said. "The proportions seem all wrong, or maybe the composition needs shift—"

"Well, *I* love it!" Ginger threw her arms around his neck and squeezed hard, then pulled back to look at the sketch again. "Look at the detail! How could you remember so much about my costume from that one time?"

"Trade secret," he said, warmed by her praise. How could he admit to her that he remembered everything about her? That tiny indentation to the left of her mouth, a scar from the chicken pox she'd had when she was five. That small cowlick at the base of her hairline that showed only when she swept her hair on top of her head. Did he have the eye of an artist, or was he just in love?

The bell rang for first period, and Linc and Ginger pushed into the foyer, shoulder to shoulder with the other students. Linc squeezed Ginger's hand as they reached the split in hallways. He watched her glide down the humanities wing, her slightly turned-out gait carrying her easily

23

through the crowd. On some ballet dancers it was almost a duck waddle. On Ginger, it was as graceful as those toe-heel steps across a stage.

After she'd disappeared through a door, Linc sighed wistfully. Then he turned and walked past the display case where the school's athletic trophies—many of them engraved with Chan's name—sat, gilded and mocking.

DON'T FORGET SALUTE TO "CHAN THE MAN" NIGHT. DECEMBER 21ST GAME! a huge banner proclaimed. BE THERE! How was their family ever going to be normal when the town couldn't forget that his dad had once been a football hero?

Inside the case stood a four-foot high state championship trophy and a silver-framed picture of "Chan the Man" as he carried the winning touchdown over the goal to snatch victory from Glory High's dreaded enemy, Meade High School, in the town just twenty miles away. Chan and his victory were legend at Glory. It was hard for Linc to fail to develop into an athlete at the site of his father's victories, and especially hard to see the trophy every day. It was dated the year he'd been born.

The picture of Chan in full gear, the ball clutched to his chest, one arm out to ward off a tackler, and a snarling expression on his face, looked out at Linc. He felt an urge to make a face back, but suddenly smiled as the football disappeared and a mangled garbage can took its place.

"Hustle, hustle, hustle, Chandler!" It was Coach Geary, standing at the gym door. "Get your butt in here and dress out, and be swift about it, or it's fifteen demerits for lateness."

Linc hurried into the locker room, where only a few stragglers were still wrestling with their laces.

"Lincoln, my man, you are gonna get in such trouble!"

Bobby Whitaker teased. He was no more than two steps ahead of Linc, himself.

"Yeah, yeah," Linc said, grinning. "Right behind you." Linc liked Bobby. He was, if anything, even more inept at P.E. than Linc, but he acted as if he couldn't care less. He made jokes about it, in fact.

Slipping hurriedly into his T-shirt and navy shorts, Linc jammed his sneakers on, hopping toward the door on one foot, then the other, as he yanked the laces taut and made an effort to tie them.

"Outside, *gentlemen*," the coach was yelling, drawing groans and protests that reverberated off the smooth walls and floors. "It's a *warm* forty-six degrees. If you keep moving, you'll be sweating in no time! Around the track six times, then to the field for some push-ups and deep knee bends. Hustle, hustle, hustle!" he yelled as he slid the maroon and white Glory "gimme" cap over his bald spot.

Linc jumped in place until his teeth stopped chattering from the sudden change in temperature. When he felt warmer, he pushed off onto the dirt track into the middle of the jam of guys, who were still groaning and complaining. Soon he was a little ahead of the pack, and concentrating on the sound of his running shoes as they hit the ground and on the rhythm of his own labored breathing.

He wasn't bad at track. But he wasn't so good that he could make his father happy. *Breathe, thump, breathe, thump.* He was only average, and average wasn't good enough for "Chan the Man."

"Chandler!" It was the coach again. "Six laps are *enough*, Chandler. Hustle, hustle, hustle!"

Linc slowed his pace gradually and looked around him. he was the only one still on the track. How many times had he gone around? His calves ached. His ankles felt prickly and on fire, and his breath came in sharp jabs. Sweat had beaded above his lip, behind his knees, and in his armpits. He suddenly felt chilled.

"Push-ups, Chandler. Hustle, hustle, hustle!"

Linc dropped to the ground. It felt cold and brittle beneath him. *Up, down, up, down, up, down.*

The coach was standing over him. "Sometimes it's hard to believe that this skinny, no-talent runt is the son of 'Chan the Man.' Faster, Chandler, faster!"

Up-down, up-down, up-damn Chan, anyway. Why did Chan have to be so revered at Glory? And why did *he* have to be "Chan the Man" 's son? At the very least, why couldn't he have been a lousy, singleminded slob of a jock like his dad?

Why did he ever have to be born?

4

LINC knew something was up the moment he got home that afternoon. Immediately he figured that his folks had found out about their kids' conspiracy to get Betty a date. But he figured in that case Betty would've found a way to warn him, or she'd be sitting at the kitchen table dissolved in tears.

Although Chan hadn't gotten home yet, his mother started her nervous banter the second Linc shut the door to the kitchen.

"Your father has a wonderful idea, Linc," she said as she shoved a plate of Linc's favorite carrot-pineapple muffins, her own creation, into his hands. She turned toward the fridge and poured a glass of milk. "And I want you to seriously consider it."

Linc sank into one of the chairs at the Formica table. The muffins were so warm they had heated the plate. He set the plate down and looked questioningly at his mother. Any time his father had a "wonderful" idea, it meant trouble for Linc. "*Consider* it, Mom? Will I have a choice? Have I *ever* had a choice when it came to Dad, I mean really a *choice*?" Linc eyed the muffins suspiciously. They were a bribe.

Polly's hands fluttered like the wings of an injured bird

as she explained. "Your father is taking a week off from the sporting goods store between Christmas and New Year's. It'll be deer season, you know."

Linc let his breath out in relief. A whole week with his father away. A whole week to not have to walk on eggs in order to not offend him. His only regret was that some poor unfortunate deer would have to die so they could have a week of peace. At least the legal limit on the deer was two. Linc broke off a piece of muffin, releasing the pent-up steam, and shoved it into his mouth. He allowed it to roll over his tongue.

"He wants you to go with him."

The muffin turned sour in Linc's mouth. "Oh, Mom, no!" He had no desire to kill or eat deer, and he certainly didn't want to be alone with Chan for a week. Of course, it might be a chance to make his father proud of him, finally, but at what price to himself? And why should he think that this would be different from any other time with his father?

Placing her hand on Linc's shoulder, Polly spoke softly, pleadingly. "Don't say no without considering it, Linc. It would be good for you two to do something together, to maybe come to know each other."

Linc could feel the tension in her fingers as her grip tightened on his shoulder. "I *know* him now, Mom. And he knows me. That's our trouble."

"I want you to know your father the way I do, to see him away from the pressures and problems that make him so—" Her hand dropped away, and she slumped into the dinette chair across from Linc with a shrug. "Linc, it would mean so much to him."

Linc figured he knew his father as well as anyone, as well as he *wanted* to know him. He remembered when, at age ten, he'd come home with a new T-shirt with a picture of a deer aiming a rifle at a hunter. ARM DEER, GIVE THEM A FIGHTING CHANCE, it had said. Linc had bought it with his allowance, picked it out himself. He'd thought it was funny.

His father had made him take the shirt back. Then he'd gone into a tirade about how hunters actually helped to weed out the weak animals from the herds before they died of starvation, as if he were on some errand of mercy, for crying out loud.

"I've never seen a hunter look for a *sick* deer to stuff on his wall," Linc had remarked.

"He's just a boy, Chan." Polly had tried to intercede. "He'll learn."

Chan had sent Linc to his room to think about his attitude. But even with his door shut he could hear his father yelling at his mother. "The kid's mocking the job that keeps us in food and clothes. You let him fall for all that Bambi crap. Where would you and the kids be if people stopped buying guns?" he'd raged. Then he'd started in on his more familiar line, about how he'd ruined his chances at a football career, taking care of her and the baby, etcetera.

Linc had hidden in his closet and cried himself to sleep. He didn't want to learn about guns, not if it meant being like his father.

"Linc," Polly said, bringing him back to the present. "I want you and your father to become close. It would mean so much to me if you'd agree to go with him, if you'd at least *pretend* to be excited about it. He's reaching out to you, Linc; don't turn away."

"I don't want to do this in the very worst way," Linc said, pushing away the plate of muffins.

"I know that, Linc," his mother said. "But you won't regret it, I promise you. You won't regret it."

He regretted it already. "I've got to think about this

awhile, Mom. I've got to think it through by myself." If he really had a choice, he wanted to understand exactly what the consequences would be if he accepted.

Polly smiled. "I understand." She patted his arm. "I'll put these muffins away for later. You think about going with your father, dear, about how happy he'll be. How happy that will make me. But don't let on to your father that you already know. He wants to surprise you." She smiled at him. "After all, it's Christmas! Get into the spirit."

Linc hardly believed that this was what Christmas spirit was about, but how could he argue with her? He carried his books up to his room. Don't let on to Chan, indeed! He set his books on his oak desk and hung his coat on the hook. Chan had probably *hoped* Mom would spring the surprise, smooth the way for him. Walking over to his window, he drew back the curtain and looked into the street below. The eight-year-old twin boys from next door and a couple of other kids Linc didn't know were playing touch football under the watchful eye of the twins' father.

Was he the only guy in America who was so different? Linc wondered. Idly, he picked up the sketch pad with the attempted family portrait. No wonder he couldn't draw himself in there. He didn't belong there.

A tap on the door jarred him loose from his thoughts. "It's me, Betty. Can I come in?"

Betty was wearing a green print tunic and pants set that their mother had designed and sewn. The color made her hazel eyes take on a green hue. Or maybe they just sparkled because she was so happy. "I told Jeffrey today that I could go with him. But I didn't say anything about you. I feel so deceitful, Linc. I mean, I'm fooling him, sort of, and Mama and Dad. I'm a jumble of nerves. But I adore him! I'm so excited!"

Linc grinned at her. She looked three years old, with her still-chubby cheeks, yet twenty, too. "You say Jeffrey is a good guy. So we'll hold off springing me on him, okay? I have a plan that's surefire. So leave it to me, okay?"

Betty danced something like a jig in place. "I'm so excited, I can't stand it!"

"Well, you'd better come down off cloud nine, or the folks will get suspicious. You've never been so excited about tagging along with me before, baby sis—. Oh, pardon me, you're not a *baby* anymore, are you?"

"Have I ever told you that I think you are not *too* awful for a big brother?" Betty said before skipping out the door.

Linc laughed—then reality hit again. He was supposed to be thinking about the hunting trip with his dad. Why hadn't his father just marched in and told him he was going to have to go with him? Did Linc really have a choice? What would life be like if he turned his father down?

He'd seen Chan in sulky moods before. It'd probably be miserable for everybody. If he accepted, only he would be miserable. And maybe his mother was right. Maybe his father was reaching out to him in the only way he knew. Could he afford the luxury of rejecting his father? But he didn't want to go with Chan—anywhere!

"Supper, Linc, Betty!" Polly was calling from downstairs. Linc heard Betty thumping down the steps, probably two at a time.

At supper, Chan seemed unusually cheery for a change, but Polly looked like a bundle of nerves. She dropped her fork twice, even spilled her glass of water on the tablecloth, although she said very little. When dinner was over, she pulled the plates practically out from under them and whisked off to the kitchen, telling Betty to help.

Linc started to rise, but his father guided him back into his chair with a firm grip on his shoulder.

Oh, boy, Linc thought, here it comes.

"I got my Christmas present from Mr. Mackey yesterday," Chan said. Mr. Mackey was the owner of the sporting goods store Chan managed and a big Glory Tigers booster. "A hunting lease out in west Texas, about six hundred miles from here."

Linc swallowed hard. "Gee." He felt like a fool, but he didn't know what else to say.

"And it gave me a great idea, Linc. I'd like you to come with me deer hunting, you know, just us *men*." His skin was blotchy, and his eyes were puffy and red, but there was still a trace of the good-looking man Polly Lincoln— and half the female population of Glory, according to the gushy notes in the yearbook—had fallen for.

"Gee."

"I want to get you fully equipped, of course. Get you down to the store and pick out some gear—hunting rifle, bedroll, jumpsuit, boots, you know." He leaned back and rubbed his chest. "My Christmas present to you."

Linc just looked at his father.

Chan grimaced slightly. "Pol," he called, "you got any of those antacid tablets? Your food didn't agree with me tonight."

"Sure," Polly said, and scurried through the swinging door. "You've been complaining a lot lately, Chan. Maybe you ought to see the doctor," she said, unwrapping the roll and placing it at his elbow.

"Maybe you ought to see a cookbook!" he snapped. He took two tablets from the roll and chewed briefly. Suddenly he leaned forward, smiling, and punched Linc on the arm, sending shock waves up into his shoulder. "Well, what do you say, son?"

Son? Suddenly he was "son." What *could* he say? "Swell." His dialogue belonged strictly to a TV sitcom, he realized. But he felt numb. Until he'd heard himself agreeing, he hadn't been sure what he was going to say.

Linc wondered if he wasn't just making up for the scam he and Betty were about to pull off. Perhaps. But for such a little prank, it seemed a high price to pay.

5

LINC dragged himself through school the following day. He was bored by the droning reviews for finals and wished it were all over. Yet he also wished it would never end. For when it did, he was going to be a dutiful son and meet his father at the sporting goods store.

"You're not eating," Ginger told him. "You'll make yourself sick if you don't eat." She straightened his collar over his sweater vest and patted it down as she spoke. If his mother had done that, he'd have been enraged. He grinned at Ginger.

The cafeteria was noisy, with the slamming of trays, clinking of flatware, and every student, it seemed, trying to shout above the din.

Linc pushed the cubed carrots and peas around on his plate. "I feel as if I'll make myself sick if I *do* eat." Quickly he filled her in on the hunting plans. "Ginger, when the last bell rings this afternoon I'll have to go to my dad's store and be outfitted like a jerk in all that stupid-looking hunting junk. Then he'll stick a gun—"

"Deer rifle," Ginger corrected, smiling. "You'll want to refer to it correctly and impress him with your knowledge and enthusiasm, won't you?"

"Yeah. He'll stick a deer rifle in my hand and call me a man. That's when I'll feel less like one than ever, I'm sure."

"It's tradition," Ginger said before putting a piece of chicken in her mouth. She spoke as she chewed. "Guys think it's macho to hunt down an animal, like the cavemen."

Linc bristled. "I'm a *guy*, and I say it stinks! Does that make me less a man than the others? Besides, if they wanted to be like the cavemen, they'd go out with a club and give the animals a fighting chance. And they call themselves *sportsmen*."

"You talk like a vegetarian, but that's a piece of beef on your plate, Linc. Have you convinced yourself that beef grows on trees? How much chance do you think that steer had? You want to know how it met its end?"

"No!" Linc said. "I don't want to know. So I'm weak and crave more protein that I can get any other way. I've seen a deer up close, at the zoo. Maybe I'd feel the same way about cows if I ever really thought about it, really looked it in its big brown eyes." He grinned. "I don't know, maybe I am a sissy. I can't help how I feel, and I resent having someone try and make me feel different." God, even Ginger thought he was a wimp.

The bell rang, and Linc took his tray to the return bin. "Will I see you this afternoon?" he asked Ginger, who followed with her tray. He was secretly hoping for an excuse to delay going to his father's store. "Get a soda, maybe neck?"

Grinning, Ginger shook her head. "I've got rehearsal just as soon as the cast can get to the city auditorium. We're doing a full-dress straight through today, so maybe I can talk to you tonight." Ginger shoved her tray into the bin and grabbed Linc's hand. "Hang in there, Linc. Something good will come out of all this, you'll see."

Linc squeezed her hand. "Yeah," he said. "Could be."

They walked out of the cafeteria arm in arm. "Just be yourself, Linc," Ginger whispered. "I love the you that you are."

A rush of warmth engulfed Linc, and he was filled with such tender feelings that he felt almost dizzy. To be loved for the person you were was intoxicating. He wanted to tell her he loved her, too, but the words hung in his throat. Maybe his parents had loved each other once. Or at least they had thought so. No, he couldn't bring himself to say it.

"Move along, you two! We have to get to class, too, you know." It was Dink, grinning broadly.

Linc gave Dink a friendly punch on the arm, then said good-bye to Ginger. "Call me when rehearsal's over if you can, okay?" He dropped back a step and turned to Dink. "Ready for that history final tomorrow? I'm so full of facts that they're starting to jumble."

"Yeah?" Dink said. "Well then, maybe you'd like to jumble my mind a little, huh? How about a study session this evening, okay?"

Linc shrugged. "Why not? I guess I could spend my time in worse ways."

Dink made a face. "Thanks a lot, pal. I think I'd feel put down if you didn't look as if your mind's on something else."

Linc smiled. He and Dink had been best friends since kindergarten, and most of the time they didn't have to say anything. Each just knew how the other was feeling.

As they strolled toward their classes, Linc told Dink about the hunting trip. "Come with me to the store after school, okay? Then we can go study."

Dink rolled his eyes. "No way! That's the sorta thing

that's just between a father and son. You know, as sacred as that little talk about the birds and bees. *Bzzzzzz.*"

"Jerk," Linc said, laughing. It had been worth a try, although Dink was right. He could just imagine his father's reaction if Dink showed up, too.

"You bet!"

"Come over about eight, okay? That'll give us two hours to brush away the cobwebs and stuff some history into that brain."

Linc stared at the sign above the sporting goods store for a minute or two before taking a deep breath and entering. It was nearly as cold inside as out. They sure weren't wasting any overhead on heat. "I'm looking for my dad, Chan—uh, Mr. Chandler," Linc told the salesman who stepped in front of him as he headed toward the back of the store, to Chan's office.

Linc wondered if the man had worked at the store a long time, or if he was there as Christmas help. He felt a slight pang of guilt for not stopping by the store more often—but only a slight pang. The more he saw his father, the more chances there were to make him angry.

The man, whose plastic name tag said *Morris Olsen*, flushed slightly as he looked toward the office. "It would be better if you waited a few minutes before going in. Mr. Chandler is, uh, in conference at the moment."

A muffled, gravelly voice rose and fell behind the lacquered office door. "You should've canceled the order. What are we going to do with baseballs at Christmas? I made you manager, and I can make you janitor, so shape up!"

Manager! He had to be talking to Chan, and he was doing so as if Chan were a naughty, stupid child.

"Yessir, I know, sir, I'm sorry, sir." That voice was his

father's, and it was uncharacteristically humble. "It won't happen again." He'd never heard Chan talk like that, and Linc thought he liked it even less than the crackle and pop of Chan's insults.

Linc cringed as the door opened. "You bet it won't, Chandler." A man who looked maybe ten years older than Linc's father pushed past Linc and the salesman without a glance of acknowledgment toward them. Linc was sure it was Mr. Mackey, the owner of the store, although Linc hadn't seen him in a long time.

Chan came out of the office, mopping sweat from his face and neck. "Mitzi," he barked at the silver-haired woman behind a central desk and cash register, "do you have any more of those antacid tablets?" Suddenly his eyes focused on Linc, and his expression changed to one of delight. He rubbed his chest slightly and said, "Later," to her.

Linc remembered seeing Mitzi at the store, even as a kid. He figured she must have come with the building.

"Linc, come on back to the hunting gear. Morris, Mitzi, this is my boy, my son Linc." Linc thought he detected a hint of pride in Chan's voice. Was it as easy as that? Be more like him, and he'd love you?

Chan patted Linc on the back and ushered him toward the rear of the store, where rows of shockingly bright orange vests and jumpsuits hung along one wall. The hanger clanged as Chan yanked a vest off and instructed Linc, "Put this on. Let's see if it's a fit."

Linc sighed and shoved his arms into the sleeve holes. He felt stupid. "Why orange? I thought you were supposed to wear camouflage stuff, you know, like the trees and bushes."

Chan threw back his head and laughed heartily. Still, Linc had the feeling that Chan was laughing *with* him, for a change. "That's a good way to get shot yourself. Naw, you want orange so the other hunters can see you're not a deer. It isn't going to matter to the deer what you wear."

Chan jammed a deerstalker cap of orange polyester onto Linc's head, then wheeled him to face a full view mirror. "Looks great, huh."

"Great."

"What are you, about five seven?" Chan rummaged through a line of jumpsuits.

"Eight." Weren't fathers supposed to know that kind of thing about their kids? His mother still had Linc and Betty back up to the rule of the broom closet to be measured at least once a year.

"Huh?"

"Five eight, Dad."

"Here, try this one on," Chan said.

"I'm sure it's fine."

"No, go on and try it. I don't want to have to bring it back. I get enough of that guff from customers."

Linc slipped into one of the small dressing rooms and put on the jumpsuit over his regular clothes. Did he give a hoot whether it fit? He just wanted to get out of there.

"That's fine," Chan said when Linc hesitantly pushed through the curtain. "Show Mitzi and Morris. Hey, look at my boy, Lincoln."

Linc could feel himself growing warm. He wasn't used to this. He stared at his feet.

"Oh, yeah! Boots. What size do you wear?"

"Nine and a half medium."

Chan ran his hand along the stacks of closed boxes that lined the wall. "Here. These are nine and a half mediums."

"Dad, I—"

"Just sit down and try them on, Linc. I want to be sure

they fit. And don't worry about the cost. These are your Christmas gifts, and I can give myself a nice discount, you remember. What's the good of being a manager if I can't do this?"

Linc untied his sneakers and jammed his feet into the boots. Mitzi and Morris were standing beside Chan, nodding their approval. "I feel like Rambo," Linc said unenthusiastically.

"Yeah!" Chan said cheerily. If he noticed how unhappy Linc was, he gave no indication. "And now come on back here."

He picked up a deer rifle and laid it tenderly in Linc's hands. "I picked it myself," he said. "A two-seventy, a slightly scaled-down model with shorter barrel and stock, but it can group inside two inches at a hundred yards."

Linc had no idea what his father was talking about, but he went to his standard answer. "Gee."

"I went through the whole shipment until I found the perfect one. Feel how balanced it is. Semi-automatic. You can get off nine shots without reloading. Wham, wham, wham! No cocking or anything. Just wham, wham! I put one of my old scopes on it. Hope you don't mind. It's forty millimeter. I didn't see any need to invest in new glass when this one's good enough for a beginner."

"Wow."

"See that target on the wall? Give it a try. If you need the preset trigger pull redressed, I'll get someone to fine-tune it."

More gibberish. Linc turned toward the target. It wasn't a regular circular target. It was the head of a stag with the circles and bull's-eye superimposed on it.

"Take aim at it. Go on, now. Put the stock against your shoulder and look through the sight."

Linc felt numb all over. He winced as his father jammed the rifle butt into his shoulder. "Take aim, now. Right at the bull's-eye, okay?"

The rifle felt heavy, and it was hard to hold it straight.

"Pull the trigger, smoothly now. Easy, isn't it? 'Course, there would be a big jolt when you really fire it. But don't worry, you'll get used to it. Knock a bruise in your shoulder, if you're not careful." He laughed heartily and slapped Linc on the back. "Knock you right out of your socks!"

In a mirror next to the target, Linc caught the image of himself and his father. He squeezed the trigger. It clicked.

Linc dropped the rifle to his side. He didn't even recognize his own image in the mirror.

He didn't want to either.

6

THE doorbell rang, and Linc hurried to answer, grateful that Dink was his usual punctual self.

Dink slipped inside and shrugged out of his jacket and tugged off his knit cap. "Man, it's cold out there. Even the dog and cat are cuddling tonight." He slung his jacket and cap onto a chair, where they landed in a rumpled pile. "Hi, Mrs. Chandler. Nice tree. Except, doesn't it need something at the top?"

"It's a family tradition for Chan to top the tree," she told him as she scooped up his jacket and cap and hung them in the guest coat closet.

"C'mon," Linc said, "let's get to the books."

Polly Chandler glanced over her shoulder at them. "Wouldn't you boys like to take some cheese and fruit to study with? I'll make up a tray and bring it up."

Linc was about to refuse, but Dink accepted before he could get the words out.

Linc's face must've mirrored his thoughts, because Dink grinned at him. "You know the rules, man. Never miss an opportunity to eat, drink, or pee. It's un-American!" He called toward the kitchen, where Polly was already opening

and closing cabinet doors. "I'll just wait and carry up the tray, Mrs. C. That'll save you the trip, okay?"

Linc crossed his eyes at Dink. "Apple-polisher," he teased. Dink would fit into this family a lot better than he did.

Link went upstairs. Soon Dink joined him with a tray of cheese, grapes, and apple slices. "I just didn't want your mom coming up and overhearing anything, that's all." He set the tray on the bed and closed the door.

"Overhear?" Linc said. "Overhear us studying? Yeah, the shock would probably be too much for her."

"Study, schmuddy," Dink said. He did a belly flop onto the bed, making the fruit and cheese dance on the tray. "I wanna hear the details!"

"Details?"

"Oh, cut the crapola. What happened with you and your dad at the store? I want all the gory details," Dink said. He sat up, resting his head on his bent arm.

"Ugh," Linc said. "It was as bad as I'd imagined it'd be. Imagine me dressed like Elmer Fudd on a Bugs Bunny hunt—cap with earflaps and all."

"Oh, man," Dink said. "Bummer." His shoulders shook with laughter.

"Thanks a lot for your sympathy, pal!" Yet Linc was seeing himself through Dink's eyes, and for the first time the situation seemed funny. "And the outfit—get this—is the color of tangerines. It literally glows in the dark! I look like a highway cone. All I need is writing on me that says *slow*." He laughed along with Dink. "And the rifle—" A cloud crossed his face. There was nothing funny about that.

Dink popped a grape into his mouth and chewed. "Maybe it won't be so bad. I once went dove hunting with my uncle

and dad. We didn't see a bird the whole time. We tramped through wet grass for two days and didn't find tracks or anything."

"Birds fly, dinkhead. They don't leave tracks."

"Oh, yeah. Well, anyway, we had to come home early, because I was catching an awful cold. They never asked me to go with them again."

"Hmmmm," Linc said. "That's an idea. Maybe if I catch a cold . . ." He sighed wearily. A cold wouldn't help. He'd probably have to get pneumonia to drag his dad away from a deer hunt.

"I got a question," Linc said. "What about you and Sandra? I didn't see you together at lunch."

Dink laughed. "The way you look at Ginger, you wouldn't see Santa Claus if he walked into the lunchroom. Naw, seriously, I guess we sorta broke up. The old magic was gone. We spent more time cutting each other down than cutting up. You know what I mean?"

"Yeah," Linc said. But he really didn't know. He couldn't imagine feeling that way about Ginger.

Dink laughed. "Always break up just before Christmas. It saves money."

"Maybe we'd better get to the history, pal," Dink said. "I mean, I already know it. But you're still stuck in this century."

Linc flipped through the history textbook and called out some questions until tires squealed in the driveway.

"Your dad's home," Dink said. "I'd better go."

Linc stared at the ceiling fixture. "It's okay. He'll have a few beers while Mom heats his supper, and then he'll eat. It'll be an hour yet before he even notices that his adoring family isn't gathered in the living room to watch him set the star on the Christmas tree. That's his big contribution

to getting ready every year." Then Linc remembered the scene at the store and how Chan's boss had talked to him. Now he could understand some of Chan's bad moods better.

Dink shrugged. "Count yourself lucky, sport. At least your dad's working this Christmas. Construction being what it is, mine's working only a day or two a week, so he spends his time thinking up home projects for me 'n' him."

They settled down to their studies for forty minutes before Polly called to Linc. "Telephone, Linc! Make it short. We're almost ready for the tree-topping."

"I gotta go, anyway," Dink said. "Good luck on the test. I'll see you at the Chan night celebration."

"Yeah," Linc said. "You, too."

Dink found his own way out, while Linc answered the phone. It was Ginger.

"I just got back from rehearsal, and I've got exciting news!" Ginger said. "I couldn't wait to call."

"You've gotten a scholarship to study ballet? You've been invited to perform at the White House?" Linc said, warming at the sound of her voice.

"This is exciting news for you!" Ginger said. "I showed your sketch to Madame Olga, and she wants your permission to use it as our poster and on the cover of our program. She'll need to know tonight, since they'll be printed tomorrow for distribution. She's all ready to chuck the art she'd originally planned to use, Linc. Yours is that good! Didn't I tell you?"

Linc leaned back against the wall, smiling. "Really? That's nice. Did you give her permission?"

"Linc," Ginger said, sounding a bit exasperated. "I may possess the sketch, thanks to your generous nature, but I don't own any rights to its reproduction. Madame needs your permission to use it."

45

"And if I say no?"

There was only the sound of a heavy sigh in answer.

"I was only kidding, Ginger. Sure, use it with my blessings, if she thinks it isn't too awful."

"Great! I'll call her right now. She's waiting to hear." Ginger paused. "Hey, are you okay, Linc?"

"Sure, why wouldn't I be?"

"I don't know. Your voice just sounds . . . well, kind of funny tonight. You know, distracted or something. You aren't mad at me about sharing your sketch, are you?"

"No, I think it's great. A real confidence booster."

She sighed audibly into the phone. "Oh, good. I was afraid I shouldn't have shared a personal gift. But I'm so proud of your talent, Linc." She paused. "Then it's you and your dad. The shopping trip? Was it so awful? Oh, I wish I was there with you right now."

No wonder he cared about her so much. "I'm okay, honest. I'll tell you about it later. I'll be glad when you're finished with all these rehearsals. I miss you!"

"Yeah, me, too," Ginger said. "See you tomorrow. Thanks for the permission. Love you!"

"Yeah," Linc said. "Me, too."

Linc felt light-headed as he hung up the phone. His illustration would be a poster and program cover for the ballet. It was something to brag about a little, wasn't it? A stranger liking his work enough to print it? Wait until he told his folks that. Then they'd feel differently about his art.

Linc bounded down the stairs and into the living room.

"You sound like a herd of buffalo, Linc. How many times have I said not to run in the house," Chan grumbled.

So much for his good mood. "Sorry, Dad, it's just that I heard just now that—"

"Cider and gingerbread time!" Polly Chandler called

46

cheerily as she brought a tray in and set it on the coffee table. Four Santa's-head cups steamed with spicy smells, and four gingerbread men lay still warm on paper napkins decorated with holly leaves.

"I'm afraid one of the raisin eyes fell out," Polly said apologetically to no one in particular. "It just rolled right off as I was putting the cookies on the tray."

"He looks as if he's winking," Betty said. "I'll take him."

Link thought he'd try again. "Guess wh—"

"Get yours, Linc," his mother said. "Is the cider okay, Chan? This is your mother's recipe."

"Fine, Pol," he replied. Linc was sure he'd rather it was beer.

"Guess—"

"Did Dink go home?" Polly asked.

"Who was that on the phone?" Chan said.

Linc took a deep breath. At last, he was getting his chance. "It was Ginger. And guess what she—"

"Doesn't that girl know it's after ten?" Chan said. "You should tell her not to call so late." He set down his cider mug and reached for the star decoration as he spoke. "There was a time when girls waited to be called."

"Yeah, but she wanted to tell me that my—"

"Attention, everyone." Polly said. "Your father is affixing the star to the tree. Betty, hit the light switch."

The lights came on full. "Oooooh," she said. "It's our most beautiful tree ever." She clasped her hands and looked almost misty eyed. "What a wonderful family tradition, don't you think? Linc, put down your cup now. It's time to sing."

"But—"

"Come on, everyone, sing! 'It came upon a midnight clear.' You too, Linc. 'That glorious song of old . . .' "

47

Linc glanced at Chan, who was mouthing the song but not making much sound. As he turned his gaze on Betty, she crossed her eyes as if to say that theirs was the weirdest family around. He smiled at her as the song ended. Thank goodness they never sang more than one verse, because no one could remember any more than that.

A strong charcoal smell sent Polly scurrying toward the kitchen, shrieking that her second batch of gingerbread men was probably burned to a crisp.

Chan retired to his television in the den.

Betty stacked the empty mugs on the tray, preparing to carry it into the kitchen. "Weren't you trying to tell us something a while ago, Linc?"

"Never mind," he said. "It wasn't important."

At least not to them.

7

"GRANDMA and Granddad Chandler and Grandma Lincoln will be in sometime tomorrow," Polly Chandler said at breakfast the next morning. Her father had died when she was a baby. "They're coming early enough to go to the salute to Chan." She placed a stack of pancakes in front of Linc and moved the syrup closer to him. "We'll want them to feel welcome."

"Yeah," Linc said as he watched the thick, dark syrup slide across the pancakes and curl around the edges. He glanced up at Betty, who smiled at him fleetingly. As far as they were concerned, a Christmas *without* their grandparents would be welcome. It was always a difficult time.

Mrs. Chandler continued. "I've washed the guest linens. You can put them on the beds tomorrow. I'll go over the house thoroughly tomorrow with the duster and vacuum. There's still so much to do, it's an absolute mess. And I've made up a few casseroles so I won't be in the kitchen the whole time they're here."

She was really talking to herself, cataloging what she needed to do. Linc glanced involuntarily around the kitchen. By rights it should have at least a pancake griddle in sight, or maybe a few remnants of breakfast, but it was

49

spotless, as usual. As was the remainder of the house, he was sure.

"I'll bring home a couple of logs for the fire," Chan volunteered. "It always looks so nice with the fireplace going, even though we don't need it with the central heat."

Polly brushed her hand along his neck as she passed by. "Thank you. That's a good idea."

"Anything I can do to help?" Linc asked.

"Yeah," Betty said. "Me, too."

"Thank you," their mother said. "I'll let you know. Mostly, I'll expect you two to be respectful to your grandparents and to make good grades on your semester finals today."

When their father had left the table and their mother had gone off to straighten something, Betty leaned toward Linc. "Linc, I hate to mention this again, but you haven't said any more about getting me and Jeffrey together for the ballet," she said. "It'll happen in just three days. What am I going to do? You said you'd help."

"I'll take care of it, Betty. I said I would, didn't I?" Linc's tone was sharper than he'd intended, and he saw that Betty had slumped back into her chair, obviously feeling rebuffed. He hadn't meant to hurt her. It was just that he had a lot of things going on in his head right then. He wasn't looking forward to the visit from his grandparents—or to the Christmas present from his father.

But the last day of school passed quickly, and afterward Linc stopped at a jeweler's to choose some barrettes for Ginger. Then there was little time for thinking when Linc and Betty got home. At once, their mother began marshalling their aid in readying the house for guests.

"Linc, Betty. I want you to get all the junk in your rooms cleared out of sight. Empty the top drawer in your chest of drawers, and be sure there's some hanger space in your closets."

She needn't have told them. They went through the same routine just about every year at Christmas, and one or the other of them several times a year, depending on who was visiting. Since Linc's room held a single three-quarter-sized bed, Grandma Lincoln used his room during her stays. Betty's room had twin beds, so that was where Grandma and Granddad Chandler stayed.

Linc would use the sofa bed in the living room, and Betty would use the one in the den. All in all, it worked out pretty well—for the visitors, anyway. The sofa beds certainly left something to be desired in comfort, and Linc always secretly hoped that the grandparents would not stay long. The household was always in turmoil by the time they left, and feathers were ruffled from words thoughtlessly spoken.

Linc went to his room and busied himself with the housekeeping duties until his mother called them to supper. "The first thing tomorrow morning, I want you two to put the guest linens on your beds and make sure that everything looks perfect. I don't know yet just what time your grandparents will be arriving, but we'll be prepared," Polly said as she passed the food around the table.

"I'll take care of putting fresh-cut flowers in the rooms tomorrow morning. Our pansies are lovely this time of the year and will look pretty floating in my cut crystal bowls. I think cut flowers make such a nice welcome. Maybe I should get some of that room freshener, an herbal scent or roses. Yes, that's it—roses."

The next morning, Linc drove into town. He picked up Ginger's barrettes, which he'd left at the jeweler's to be engraved with her name. Then he bought some battery-warmed socks for his father to wear on his hunting trips, a necklace of amber-colored beads for Betty, and for his mother a pair of embroidery scissors.

Back home, Linc slipped his purchases up to his room. By the time he had wrapped his packages and placed them under the tree, it was one o'clock. His mother was in the kitchen making potato salad. "Linc, would you put seven plates and silverware settings on the buffet in the dining room, please? And see that there are enough napkins out, too. Now, don't just stick them on the buffet, Linc. Make them look, you know, festive."

Linc glanced at the table and saw that his mother had put out a red tablecloth with white snowflake appliqués, her own design. He pulled the matching napkins from the buffet drawer and arranged them in a fanlike shape with knives, forks and spoons on top. He pulled the white plates from the buffet cabinet and set them next to the napkins.

Soon his mother bustled in and ran her hands over his arrangement, flicking a fork one way and a spoon another. She might as well have done it herself. She was never satisfied with anything he did.

She moved the flower arrangement from the buffet, where he'd set it, to the center of the table.

"It looks pretty, Mom," Linc told her.

"You think so? I don't know. Maybe I should put the snowman in the center instead of the flowers, to go more with the tablecloth, do you think?"

"It's nice just the way you have it, Mom. Everything's going to be great." He was beginning to understand Ginger's impatience with his own lack of confidence.

"Maybe I should've used the green tablecloth with holly."

"No, Mom. It looks really nice."

The doorbell rang. "Answer the door, Linc," she told

him. "Don't keep your grandparents waiting out there in the chill."

Grandma Chandler was retying the bow on the door wreath when Linc opened the door. She looked well tanned, almost leathery, and the bright yellow sweats she was wearing made her stand out like sunshine against the gray day. She wore no makeup, but looked ruggedly healthy. She smiled broadly. "Hello, Lincoln. You've grown another foot since we last saw you."

He hadn't grown even a full inch since Easter, when they were last there, but he enjoyed hearing that he had.

"But you look so pale! Don't you ever get any sunshine here anymore?" She leaned forward to give Linc a quick hug and peck on the cheek. "Granddad will be along in a second. He's getting the luggage," she said.

"Come on in, Grandma," Linc said. "I'll help Granddad."

By that time, his mother was at the door, taking Grandma's coat and making small talk about the trip over from Tucson, where they had retired when Granddad left his sportscasting job.

Linc ran out to the car and shook hands with his grandfather. Then they hugged briefly, patting each other on the back. "I'll get those suitcases, Granddad," Linc offered. "You go on in."

"Nonsense, Linc!" his grandfather said. "I still pump iron every day and jog five miles. You think I can't handle a few little suitcases? Of course, Leona always packs more than she needs for a trip." Deftly he pulled the two suitcases from the trunk. Linc shut the trunk before running ahead of his grandfather to hold the front door open.

"Linc!" His mother scolded him the moment they'd gotten into the house. "Why didn't you carry the luggage for Granddad?"

Linc shrugged, holding his hands, palms up, in surrender. He could make Granddad mad by making him feel as if he were a helpless old man, or he could offend his mother by looking like a lazy slob. There was no right way in this house.

"Same room as before, Polly?" Granddad asked.

"Yes, Dad," Polly said. "Let Linc take those up for you, though."

"Nonsense, Polly. I pump iron every day, and I jog five miles. These little suitcases are nothing to a hunk like me." He strode up the steps and vanished from sight.

"Oh, Linc," Grandma said, "you can do something to help. There's a big box in the backseat of the car that's filled with Christmas presents. If you'll bring that in, I'd appreciate it, dear." She stretched tall, then bent and touched her toes. "Feels good to loosen up."

Linc got the box, and Grandma placed the wrapped presents under the tree, then gave the box to Linc to throw away. When Linc returned, Grandma took hold of his chin and turned his face to the left, then to the right. "Stand there a minute, Lincoln," she said. "Let me take a good look at you!" She backed to arm's length. "You certainly are maturing into a fine young man. You'll be overtaking your dad pretty soon."

She turned to Polly. "He gets better looking every time I see him, but I can't see any resemblance to you or Clarke."

Linc smiled wryly. He knew he didn't look like either of his parents, but he was beginning to realize that he wasn't so different from his mother.

Linc imagined the Chandlers' fury when their son married in his senior year and dropped out of college after a year to support a baby nobody had wanted. He could hear the Chandlers asking Chan, "Are you *sure* the baby's yours?" Did they still wonder sometimes? Did they still regret Chan's lost career, even as Chan did?

"I'll have some lunch ready in a few minutes. I hope you don't mind a light one, since it's so late," Linc's mother said. "Just sit down and relax. You must be exhausted from the drive."

Grandma said, "A light lunch is just fine with us, Polly. We eat lightly. Eat like a king at breakfast, a duke at lunch, and a pauper at supper, the saying goes. Our cholesterol counts are A-OK, and our physicals show we're in peak condition." She took a deep breath and let it out slowly, deliberately. "What I'm exhausted from is *sitting*, Polly."

She did a couple of deep knee bends before speaking again. "Let me help you. I need to move about a bit and unkink some of these muscles." She had changed a lot from the grandma Linc remembered from his youth. She seemed to have more self-confidence. Had it been a gradual thing or an overnight miracle? If she was a "late bloomer," maybe there was a chance for himself—even for his mom.

The two women headed for the kitchen, and Linc stood in the middle of the living room, feeling suddenly like a stranger in his own house.

8

GRANDDAD bounded down the stairs, giving Linc's shoulder a friendly shake. "Let me take a look at you, Linc. You've really grown this last year, but you don't seem to be getting much meat on your bones. Are you working out? You should work out, you know. I lift weights and jog five miles a day."

He was in the kitchen before Linc could answer. Linc followed him and leaned against the door frame, listening. "Got any coffee, Polly? Leona won't let me stop for coffee on the road. It's the one indulgence I've hung on to, although she's trying hard enough to break me of the nasty habit." He laughed.

"Me?" Grandma said. "Why, Polly, don't you believe a word of it. It's Bronson who won't stop. Once he gets into that car, he's determined to make it in one sweep. Macho motor man. Heaven help us if we have to travel farther than a tank of gas will carry us."

"That's why we buy big cars. They stick to the road, and they hold a lot of gas. Where's Clarke?" Granddad asked as he sipped the coffee Polly had poured for him. "I'll bet he's not Christmas shopping. Does he still wait until the last minute? He's not *working* on a Saturday, is he?"

"Just a half day, Dad," Polly said. "Since he became the manager of the store, his hours have stretched."

Granddad sniffed. "The boss should be able to set his own hours. If he'd just had a few years in the pros, he could've gotten a broadcast job, the way I did."

"And where is our beautiful granddaughter?" Grandma asked. Linc was sure he'd seen Grandma step hard on Granddad's foot.

"Finishing up her Christmas shopping," Polly replied. "You know Betty. She'll look at everything in the mall and downtown twice before she decides what she's buying." She laughed.

The doorbell rang. "I'll get it," Linc volunteered.

Grandma Lincoln was retying the bow on the door wreath. That ribbon was going to be worn out before Christmas.

She pressed her hair into place with one gloved hand and tugged at the jacket of her dusty mauve suit with the other. "Merry Christmas, Lincoln."

"Merry Christmas, Grandma." Linc scrambled to keep from dropping the purse she handed him.

She slid her gloves off and slipped them into the purse as she stepped inside, and, holding Linc's shoulders lightly, she quickly kissed him on each cheek. An almost over-powering sweet odor stung his nostrils as he inhaled.

Turning her back toward Linc, she shrugged slightly, and Linc finally realized she expected him to help her take off her suit jacket. Still juggling the purse, he held the jacket at the collar while she slipped from it, then hung it and the purse on the hall tree.

Grandma straightened the tie of her pink silk blouse and sighed as she looked about her. "Where is everyone, Lincoln?"

"In the kitchen, Grandma. I'm sure they didn't hear you, or they'd have come out to greet you."

"Um, yes. Get my luggage and the packages from my car and lock it, Linc."

He hurried out to the car as she instructed, and when he returned she was in the kitchen. Linc set the packages under the tree and carried her luggage up to his room.

By the time he got back downstairs, both Betty and Chan had arrived. They were exchanging greetings in the now crowded, humid kitchen. Linc frowned slightly at Betty, then motioned his head, indicating that she should follow him.

He walked into the living room and squatted by the tree, rearranging packages. Betty squatted beside him. "What's up?"

"I think I got this Jeffrey thing all figured out," Linc said. "It'll probably be easier with the grandparents here, keeping everybody busy and all. When I give you the go-ahead, call Jeffrey and ask him if I can hitch a ride with you. Tell him my car broke down at the last minute, and I'm stuck."

Betty looked at Linc, frowning. "Your car, Linc? Gee, I'm sorry."

He shook his head in exasperation. "It isn't really, noodlehead. But it'll look as if it is by the time it needs to be."

"Ooooh," Betty said, nodding. She smiled. "Did I ever tell you what a great—"

"Forget it, sis," he told her. "But someday I'll want a return on this favor, got it? I mean, a man doesn't harm his car lightly."

Betty reached over and squeezed his hand. "Just one more thing."

Linc rolled his eyes. "Will your demands never stop, woman?"

She snickered. "No, really. I need your opinion. Which would look better—you know, more mature—that red silk dress or the green velvet one? I mean, the red would be great for Christmas Eve, but the lace sailor collar is kinda babyish. And the green one is okay, but the velvet is kinda worn shiny where I sit on it."

Linc frowned at her. "How would I know? Ask a girl-friend!"

Betty's eyebrows rose, and her lower lip quivered slightly. "It's just that you have such an artistic eye. And you know what boys like."

"Oh," Linc said, shrugging. "Well, either take the collar off the red or hang the velvet in the bathroom when you shower. The steam ought to take some of the shine off. It works with my wool trousers, anyway."

Betty reached over and gave him an appreciative hug.

"Cut that out!" Linc said. "You want to ruin my reputation as a brother?"

"Lunch!" Polly Chandler called. "Hurry up, kids. We're all waiting."

Linc and Betty glanced guiltily at each other, then joined their family.

The "light lunch" Mrs. Chandler had mentioned turned out to be slices of honey-cured ham, fresh-baked bread, and a medley of salads from potato to molded cucumber, all arranged on the buffet. The flowers his mother had worried so about had been replaced with a miniature Christmas tree. And after all their discussion about the red tablecloth versus the green one, she'd settled on a white tablecloth with appliquéd Santa heads. Linc was beginning to feel that he came by his wishy-washiness honestly.

"The food looks delicious, Mom," Linc said. His mother had really outdone herself on what was supposed to be a casual lunch.

"Thank you, Linc," she replied, glancing at the others. "It's just some last-minute throw-togethers."

It was the conversations, not the food, that spoiled Linc's appetite every time his extended family got together. "How's business, Bea?" Granddad asked as he always did. "Just so-so?" Then he laughed and said, "Get it, Bea? Sew sew? Ouch! Watch your foot, Leona."

Grandma smiled. "Was that your leg, dear? I thought it was the table leg. Sorry."

Linc stuffed a forkful of potato salad into his mouth to keep from laughing out loud. She really *had* changed.

If Grandma Lincoln didn't get Granddad's corny jokes by now, she had to be the densest of people. Linc figured Granddad hadn't found a new joke in all these years.

In a polite but somewhat chilled tone, Beatrice Lincoln said, "Business is wonderful, Bronson. I've added two assistants but still must turn away clients."

"I don't wonder," Grandma Chandler cooed, a little too patronizingly, maybe. "You design beautifully, Bea. I should get you to make me some clothes one of these days."

Grandma obviously got her nose out of joint because she thought they were putting her down for still working, when they had been able to retire already. She glanced fleetingly at Grandma's casual clothes. "Really, Leona, you're better off buying off the rack. I don't even stock sport fabrics, since I specialize in quite expensive clothes."

Linc braced himself for an onslaught, but to his surprise

Grandma laughed spontaneously. "You're right. Our life-style is much too casual for the kind of clothes you create. I wouldn't need something like that more than two, three times a year. I'd look silly in elegant silks, anyway, with this golf-course complexion of mine. You, on the other hand, have a regal sense of how to dress."

Betty suddenly had a coughing fit and excused herself. On her way out of the dining room, she pinched Linc on the shoulder.

He stared at his plate, not daring to speak or chew until the urge to laugh had passed.

"Uh, ready for dessert, anyone?" Polly finally interrupted, to Linc's relief.

"I guess you'll be passing up the dessert, huh, Chan?" Granddad said. "Gotta tighten up that old gut, son. I pump iron every day and jog five miles. Are you working out?"

By the time the meal was over, Linc felt as if he'd been mauled by Great Danes. Betty rejoined him, and the two of them put away the leftovers and loaded the dishwasher while the others retired to the living room for more verbal jousting.

The women were arguing about the best way to roast a turkey, and Granddad and Chan were reliving football memories. "That's quite an honor, having a football game dedicated to you and the whole night called A Salute to 'Chan the Man,' " Granddad was saying. "But then I guess you were the best they ever had at Glory High, the very best."

The two men sank into a melancholy silence, and Linc figured they were both remembering what a career Chan might have had, had he played his four or five years in college and then gone into the pros. They looked up at Linc, and he flushed.

"Will you have to make a speech or anything like that at the game tonight?" Linc asked. "I think I'd be terrified to talk in front of a stadium full of people."

"I don't think so, Linc. Just the usual hello and thanks," Chan said. "They'd rather watch the game than hear me talk."

"And the cheerleaders," Granddad said, laughing.

Linc didn't mind watching football; he rather enjoyed it. He cheered for Glory as much as anyone. But he knew his father and grandfather thought he should be a player, not a spectator.

Ginger had gotten special permission to miss the rehearsal that night in order to join Linc. Anyway, it would give her understudy a chance to work out.

Linc watched as his parents, grandparents, and Betty all slid into Granddad's Lincoln. Then he climbed into his old Chevy.

Granddad pulled up beside Linc's car, and Chan lowered his window. "We'll meet you in the stands. Don't forget. Row one on the fifty-yard line. Tigers side, of course. They have a nice section roped off for the whole family."

"See?" Granddad yelled at Linc. "Big cars have a lot of practical uses. Try and get six people into one of those little foreign jobs."

Linc was only halfway up the sidewalk at Ginger's when she dashed down the steps toward him. She slid her arm around him, and they walked arm in arm toward the car. "We have to sit in the family section tonight," Linc said apologetically.

"Ummmm, I'm with a celebrity tonight," Ginger teased. "I hope I can handle this." She nuzzled his neck as he opened the car door for her.

When she was seated and he'd shut the door, he hurried

around to his own side. As the motor hummed to life, he buckled his seat belt, then looked over at her, grinning. "You definitely look celebrity yourself tonight. Uh, the down side of all this is that you have to meet all of my ditzy relatives. Will you still care for me, once you've seen the stock from which I sprang?"

Ginger laughed. "They couldn't be any worse than mine. Did I ever tell you I have an uncle who used to get fired out of a cannon for a living?"

"You're making that up."

"Yeah, but it made you feel a whole lot better for a minute there, didn't it?"

Linc reached over and squeezed her hand. "For a minute."

9

AT the stadium, Linc got Ginger through the family introductions with few embarrassing moments. One was when Granddad said, "She's cute, Linc, and she's even skinnier than you, impossible as that sounds." That was just before he told her how he lifted weights and jogged five miles every day.

Flushing, Linc shrugged slightly. But Ginger laughed and told Granddad it wouldn't do for her to get too heavy, since she was a ballerina.

"I guess it really keeps you on your toes. Get it? Ballerina? On your toes?" Granddad said just before Grandma stepped on his foot again. Linc wondered why Granddad never seemed to catch on, considering the beating his toes took from Grandma.

The big surprise came at half time. The whole family had to traipse out onto the field with Chan while the band played the Glory fight song and a banner was lowered at the flag end of the stadium to reveal that the stadium had been renamed after Chan.

"Three generations of Chandler men in the stands tonight folks," the district superintendent said. " 'Bronson the

Brawn' Chandler and 'Chan the Man' Chandler, the pride of Glory football. And Lincoln Chandler."

Linc could feel his ears burn. 'Bronson the Brawn,' 'Chan the Man,' and 'Linc the Wimp.' Why weren't they booing and throwing tomatoes or something? What a loser!

"I'm glad the Tigers won tonight, since they dedicated the game to him, but I wanted to crawl into a hole," Linc confided in Ginger as they left the stadium and headed for Forty-Five Flavors to meet his family.

"It's kinda hard to be in the spotlight when you're not used to it, I guess. I felt the same way the first time I did a solo on stage."

"I meant all those grand introductions, then, 'Oh, yeah, and here is the unheroic third generation.'"

"Well, think about this. Betty was treated as one of 'the others' in the family."

"Oh, my gosh, you're right. I was so wrapped up in my own pity that I didn't even notice. Let's hope she didn't, either."

"Arrrrrgh. How could she not notice? Men!"

"And my grandparents. My grandfather is so corny."

"Did I ever tell you about my aunt Jessie, who thinks she's a teapot?"

"You're making that up," Linc said.

"Yeah," Ginger said, laughing.

By the time Linc had found a parking place and he and Ginger had gotten inside the ice cream parlor, patrons had recognized Chan and were giving him the royal treatment.

Betty was hanging back. Linc and Ginger scooped her between them and led her to the table. "Lemme sit in the corner here against the wall," Betty said sourly. "You guys sit on the outside."

"If you're still thinking about the lousy way the announcer introduced us tonight, Betty, I'm really sorry," Linc said.

She shrugged it off. "Just look around you. Everybody's got a date. I could die. I could just die. I don't want anyone to see me in here with my family."

"You mean you're not upset about the announcer?"

"Pfffft," Betty said. "How could I get upset when Dad is in his glory? Look at him. He's positively glowing."

Linc looked at Ginger and grinned. "When Dad's happy, we all do a lot better. Let's hope the feeling lasts."

When they had ordered, Linc thought he'd take advantage of the light-hearted mood. "Granddad, how long has it been since you've been deer hunting?"

"A couple of years, I guess. I met Clarke out in Bracketville that year. Cold as the Arctic, if I remember. Sure would like to go again, though."

"You could use my gear, Granddad, if you wanted to take my place this year. I can wait another year," Linc offered. He could wait forever, if the truth were known. He didn't dare look at Chan at that moment.

"That's very generous of you, Linc, but I wouldn't deprive you and your dad of such an experience for the world. No, sir. Besides, Leona and I are heading down to Florida on the twenty-sixth for the oldtimers' celebrity golf tournament. Wish they'd find a new name for it. Oldtimers, indeed. Did I tell you I lift weights and jog five miles every day?"

Ginger grinned at him. "I believe you've mentioned it."

"Granddad was a linebacker for the Steelers in the fifties, until he had to have both knees operated on from injuries. Then he became a radio sportscaster," Linc explained to

Ginger. Turning to his grandfather, he said, "If you change your mind, Granddad, let me know."

Linc and Ginger excused themselves. "I need to get Ginger home early," Linc said. The truth was, he didn't think he could take much more of the football talk.

The car heater had made the car warm, and the windows had frosted over quickly. The outdoor lights the Rawlingses had put up were muted eerily through the frost.

Linc shut off the motor and put his arm around Ginger's shoulder, pulling her closer. Resting his forehead against hers, he said, "You smell good tonight."

She laughed. "It's chocolate raspberry ripple. I spilled some on my sweater at Forty-Five Flavors."

"Are you cold?"

"Not as long as you keep your arms around me. You okay?"

Linc heaved a weary sigh. "I guess. I just think what with my grandparents all taking verbal jabs at one another and my folks and with the hunting trip hanging over my head, I can hardly wait for this stupid year to be over."

Ginger reached around to the back of his neck and pulled his face to hers, kissing him. Linc felt warm waves ripple over his body. "Ginger . . ."

"Shhhhh," Ginger said and kissed him again, this time harder. She leaned back, smiling at him.

"Ginger, I wish—"

The Christmas light reflections shut off and on a couple of times. Ginger put her finger to his lips. "That was a signal from my father that I've been sitting in this car with you too long and should come in," she said. "Poor dear, he's never caught on that kids don't do it in front of their own houses."

"Just a minute longer." Linc squeezed her hand, afraid to let go.

"Sorry, dear one, but I'm afraid he'll come out and jerk me from the car. I'd better get in." She gave Linc a quick peck on the cheek and slid toward the passenger door.

Linc opened his door and felt a sharp blast of cold air. He went around, opened the car door, and escorted Ginger to the porch. He squeezed her hand. "See you at the ballet."

She pulled him closer and Linc wrapped his arms around her shoulders and kissed her quickly, just in case Mr. Rawlings was watching them. When she'd closed the door, Linc hurried back to his car. He smiled. Maybe he'd been wrong, thinking Ginger was so experienced. Maybe he wasn't the only teenager in the world who hadn't done it. Maybe lots of them were just talking.

10

THE next couple of days were fairly uneventful, except that Granddad got Chan and Linc to go on a five-mile jog with him.

Out of shape, Chan was the first to slow. He was puffing hard, and he seemed to alternate between flushing and paling. He bent over, his hands resting on his knees.

Linc jogged over to him. "You okay, Dad?"

"Yeah." Chan growled. "Just my old knee injury acting up, that's all. Jogging's stupid, anyway. I gotta get ready for work."

Linc saw that his grandfather was out of sight. "Yeah, right. It's stupid, anyway. I'll walk back to the house with you." Linc pretended to be out of breath, although he was actually in pretty good shape from P.E. "Whew, I'm beat." He didn't mind making his father feel better, or giving Granddad something to brag about.

Christmas Eve morning, Linc was under the hood of his car, leaning over the motor, wiping and tightening whatever he could find. He jumped, nearly hitting his head on the hood, when Betty suddenly spoke.

"Linc, it's tonight! Jeffrey will be coming in just seven hours, twenty minutes, and ten seconds."

"I know, duffus," Linc replied.

"Huh?"

"I'm faking car trouble, get it? You called Jeffrey, didn't you?"

Betty grinned. "He was an absolute doll. He said, no problem, you can ride with us."

"See?" Linc said. "Piece of cake!" He hoped. "Just remember, when Jeffrey gets here, let *me* answer the door. It'll look more natural that way."

Obviously satisfied, Betty hurried off.

Linc smiled and continued his bogus bout with the car. "Trouble?"

Linc's head popped up, this time bumping the hood. If people didn't quit sneaking up on him, he wouldn't be at the ballet at all; he'd be in the hospital with a concussion! "Oh, hi, Dad. Yeah, I thought you'd already be at the store." Actually, Linc knew his father was still home, since he saw the jeep in the garage. That was why he started his act.

Chan leaned on the fender next to Linc. "I'm waiting for your granddad. He's going in with me this morning. I'm going to show him around the store, let him do a bit of discount shopping. We're closing up about four and we'll have a brief store party."

"That's nice."

"You want me to help while I'm waiting? Turn the motor over or anything?"

"No. Uh, thanks, Dad, but you're all dressed for the store. Wouldn't want you to get messed up or anything. I'll manage."

Chan straightened up, slapped Linc on the back, and said, "Good luck with it, son."

Chan seemed proud of him for leaning over a car motor. Linc guessed that was manly enough for his father.

Chan went off to warm up the jeep motor.

"Trouble?"

Linc jumped, dropping the wrench. It clanked against various parts of the car as gravity pulled it to the concrete below. Gee, maybe he should hang out a sign. This time it was Granddad.

"Yes, sir. Trouble." He decided to plant the second seed. "Don't know if I'm going to get it going by tonight or not."

"Oh, and your mother was telling me you were taking Betty to the ballet, too. Well, if you don't get your car going by tonight, you can use my car. We'll be staying in probably."

It sure was hard being sneaky around there. Linc's mind was racing. "That's nice of you, Granddad. But your car won't be insured for a minor driver. And if anything happened to it, I'd never forgive myself."

Granddad slapped him on the back. "You're a thoughtful boy, Linc. A good fellow."

A heel, actually. A con man. Had he found his calling at last? Now he would plant the third and final seed. "If I don't get the car fixed in time, Jeffrey will give me—us— a ride. It'll be okay. Besides, Granddad, you might want to go driving and look at the neighborhood decorations. And you know Dad's jeep isn't fit for that."

"Big cars do come in handy, don't they, Linc? It's good that you can get another ride," Granddad said. "It'd be a shame to disappoint Betty. She was in there rolling up her hair when I left the house. It's really important to her, going out with her big brother."

The jeep horn beeped, and Granddad left to join Chan.

Linc leaned on the fender of his Chevy and waved to them as they drove off. It seemed to be working out all right.

By the end of the day, Linc had put his car up on blocks. Betty was going to owe him for this favor, owe him plenty.

Chan and Granddad came back in the cheeriest of moods. A store party with spiked punch and munchies could do that, Linc guessed.

"How'd you like the store, Dad?" Polly asked Bronson. "Didn't it look nice for Christmas?"

"Dad didn't like the color paint I chose for the walls this year," Chan said between clenched teeth.

"It would look better in a toast color, sort of pigskin brown," Granddad said. "Don't you think so, Linc?"

"Oh, I don't know," Linc said, shrugging. He could see that his dad was irritated and hoped to change the subject. "I think the news is on TV, Granddad."

Bronson Chandler hurried into the den. Scowling, Chan opened the refrigerator and stood staring into it. "Nothing is ever right. Nothing. How soon is dinner, Pol?"

"I'll dish it up soon, Chan," she replied. "Linc and Betty have to eat now. We'll sit down the minute they finish. If we hurry, we can be in the living room to see them go. Betty's so excited. Isn't that cute?" Polly said as she set their plates on the table.

Oh, great. They were all going to be sitting there, inspecting them.

Betty gave Linc a nervous glance.

Sighing, Polly continued, "Well, I guess I'll join your grandmothers in the living room. They're rearranging my decorations, and each other's. Just once I'd like to feel that they approve of something."

Betty and Linc glanced at each other. Linc raised an

eyebrow and Betty shrugged in answer. Linc had never realized his mother felt that way, too.

He pushed his food around on his plate and worried about how they were going to get Betty on this date without major problems. Betty put her fork down. "I think I'm going to be sick. My stomach feels as if it's full of stones."

"Yeah?" Linc said. "Well, mine isn't in too great shape, either. I mean, if we're caught, I may never get out of this house again, and to top that my perfectly good car is up on blocks and it'll have to stay there until I get back from that stupid hunting trip."

"I owe you, Linc."

"You bet you do. Maybe you could figure a way to get me out of that trip."

Betty sighed. "I would if I could, Linc. Honest. You're the greatest, doing this for me."

"Yeah," Linc replied.

The entire family was in the living room when Jeffrey's car drove up later. Betty clutched her stomach, and Linc figured it, like his own, was tied in knots. He glanced at Betty, then jumped up.

He opened the door. "Jeffrey, good buddy! Thanks so much for the ride tonight."

Jeffrey looked a bit startled. "Uh, glad to help out, Linc." His gaze flitted around the room, landed on Betty, then seemed to melt. He grinned as she stood up.

Betty was in the green velvet dress with a wide lace collar, Victorian style. She did look terrific, Linc thought, even if she was his baby sister.

"Meet the family," Linc said. "Mom and Dad, and my grandparents, Mr. and Mrs. Chandler and Mrs. Lincoln."

Dutifully, Jeffrey shook hands with each. "Congratulations on your game honor the other evening, sir," Jeffrey told Chan.

"And of course you know Betty," Linc added as an afterthought.

The question mark came back into Jeffrey's expression. He grinned. "Yeah."

"Well, we'd better be going," Linc said, feeling as if his throat was going to close up any second.

Linc grabbed his jacket from the hall tree. Betty got hers and Jeffrey helped her with it, then ushered her out the door.

Linc looked back at his parents. "A real gentleman, huh? I should've thought of that. Well, don't wait up!" He closed the door with a silent prayer. Don't wait up, please.

"I appreciate your giving me a ride, under the circumstances," Linc told Jeffrey.

Jeffrey nodded as he closed the door on Betty's side. "That's okay. I saw your car on blocks back there. That's rough. Glad I could help."

"I'll get out of your way as soon as we get there." Linc crawled into the back seat, and Jeffrey slid in behind the wheel.

"Good. I mean, that's okay," Jeffrey said.

Linc smiled. Jeffrey didn't seem like a "hunk," as Betty had described him. But he was a nice enough kid.

Linc was a bit stunned to see his sketch of Ginger enlarged to gigantic proportions and multiplied across the front of the auditorium and in the lobby.

Betty gasped and grabbed his arm. "Linc, that poster has your signature on it! Look, Jeffrey, that's Linc's artwork. Isn't it great? Linc, why didn't you tell us?"

No one could say he hadn't tried. He shrugged. He wondered if Madame Olga had saved a few copies for him. How would it look if he ripped one off the wall after the ballet?

He left Jeffrey and Betty with a promise to meet them at the end. As he entered the auditorium, an usher put a program into his hand, and once more he saw his sketch. It wasn't bad, really. "Uh, can you give me a couple more of those?" he asked.

He saw Mr. and Mrs. Rawlings, Ginger's parents, up front and center and spoke briefly to them, then found his seat near the front. The orchestra was warming up, and the crowd was buzzing, adding to the excitement. There were a few bumps and noises from behind the curtain, probably last-minute adjustments to the scenery.

Linc patted his jacket pocket to be sure he still had the money he'd set aside. He couldn't afford to buy Ginger a dozen roses, as he would have liked, but he could get her one long stemmed rose. He'd do that at intermission; they sold them in the lobby.

The orchestra played the overture, then the curtain rose on the party scene. Ginger looked breathtaking, and her dancing was flawless. Linc realized he was smiling throughout the program, but he couldn't help it. He was so proud of her. He could feel his heart thumping in his chest.

He bought the rose at intermission and spotted Betty and Jeffrey at the juice stand. Betty glowed. He decided all the risk was worth it.

When the ballet was over, Linc met Betty and Jeffrey in the lobby. "There's a cast party in the restaurant across the street," he said. "Would you like to go for a while?"

"Can we?" Jeffrey asked. He looked at Betty with such admiration that Linc couldn't help but smile.

"Sure, we're invited by the star!" Linc said. He looked at Betty, who took the cue.

"But let's make it out of there early, okay? I mean, tomorrow is Christmas, and I'm sure we all have family activities, okay?" She was looking at Jeffrey with full attention, and he was returning the look, nodding as if she'd said something wonderful.

At the door to the restaurant, Ginger stood with her parents and some of the other cast members, shaking hands and accepting congratulations. Reproductions of Linc's sketch were posted everywhere, and Linc couldn't help but swell a bit from pride. Then he saw that Ginger was already carrying an armful of roses and felt a sudden urge to throw his small token away.

Ginger spoke briefly to Jeffrey and Betty, then said, "Linc, what have you got behind your back?"

"Not much," he said, kissing her on the cheek. Then, feeling stupid, he handed her the single flower.

She kissed him again. "This is prettier than all the rest because it's from you, Linc."

"I wish it could be a truckload, Ginger. You were absolutely sensational. I've never seen you dance as well as you did tonight."

"Oh, I felt the part completely." She took his arm and walked with him away from the receiving line. "You know what it's all about, don't you, Linc?" Her voice was coquettish, and she brushed her lips close to his ear, making him turn warm.

"Sure, I do. It's all this dream the girl has after a big party, too much excitement, sort of."

Ginger laughed. "Actually, it's about the young girl awakening to her own sexuality and fantasizing about the young soldier and her uncle."

"Yeah," Linc said, realizing she was making fun of him. "I see some people are waiting to talk with you. And it *is* your night. Maybe you'd better get back in line."

Linc stood around uncomfortably because Ginger, the center of attention, had to be shared by everyone. That was what it would be like later, too—her getting raves, him standing around like a leftover. Ginger was going to be famous one day, he knew that. Was he going to wind up a clerk at his dad's store?

Jeffrey signaled Linc, and Linc went to say goodbye to Ginger. "I'll see you tomorrow, okay? It'll have to be early, because we'll leave early the next morning for west Texas."

Ginger hugged him and kissed him again. "It's going to be all right, Linc. I just know it."

He hoped she was right.

11

LINC yawned and stretched, yearning to pull the covers up to his nose and grab another hour or even thirty minutes of sleep. But the smell of bacon and eggs drifted into the living room, and he was aware of heavy foot traffic. Everyone else was up, and that meant he'd better get up, too.

Christmas should be a great time. At least it had seemed that way to Linc when he was just a kid. Maybe that was because he hadn't been aware then of all the behind-the-scenes preparation or the competition among his parents and grandparents.

A few minutes before dinner, he excused himself to run over to Dink's with his Christmas present, a stopwatch Dink had had his eye on for a time. It was just a plastic casing, but the inner workings seemed okay. Dink gave him a pair of insulated gloves. "I guess I'll see you after the trip," Linc said gloomily.

"Man, you act as if you've been sentenced to death row or something," Dink said. "It ought to be a blast, lugging all that stuff around, sleeping on the cold ground, peeing behind a mesquite bush." He laughed heartily.

Linc joined him, despite himself. "Some friend you are.

Well, at least my hands will be warm, thanks to you." They popped each other on the arm in farewell.

Linc hurried home in the brisk, misty air. A few little kids were already outside with their shiny new bikes and some grown-up holding them as steady as possible. Multicolored lights blinked on some of the houses, and there was a hickory smell in the air from fireplaces. Linc trotted down his drive and through the door to the kitchen. "We didn't hear you two come in last night," Polly said as she pulled the turkey from the oven to let it cool awhile. Immediately it was surrounded by the grandmothers, each offering her opinion as to whether or not it was overcooked, just right, or shouldn't have been removed from the oven.

"Good," Linc said without thinking.

"What?"

"Uh, oh, I meant I'm glad we didn't wake you."

"What did you think of the ballet, Betty?" her mother wanted to know.

Betty was whipping the potatoes. She set down the whisk and hugged herself dreamily. "Oh, it was wonderful. The best time I've ever had in my life. I *loved* every minute of it."

"Goodness, Linc, you should take your sister to the ballet more often," Polly said. Leaning toward Linc, she said, "You know, I think your friend has a crush on Betty. Did you see the way he looked at her?"

Linc forced himself not to smile. "He's a nice guy, Mom. Betty could do a lot worse. It might be a good idea to let them go out some, maybe double-date to begin with."

From the corner of his eye, Linc could see Betty paying rapt attention.

"With you, you mean?" Polly asked.

"Well, uh, yeah, I guess." That would certainly throw ice on a potentially hot situation with Ginger, wouldn't it?

"We'll see," Polly said.

Betty mouthed, "I love you."

"Call everyone in to dinner, and we'll open the presents after things are put away," Polly said.

Each of the women had made her own favorite dressing, and there was no excuse accepted for not trying them and then diplomatically explaining that they were all just too wonderful to compare. Linc thought his stomach might explode by the time the grandmothers had argued them into trying little pieces of mince and pumpkin pie, too.

"Eat up, everyone," Granddad said. "There's presents to open and football games to watch. I'll skip dessert today and skip the jogging. How about you, Chan?"

Chan mumbled something no one understood and pushed back his plate. Granddad seemed to forget that Chan was a grown-up with nearly grown-up children of his own. He talked to him as he would to a child.

Linc figured he could wait just about forever to open his presents. He knew what he was getting: hunting junk. Some Christmas.

He was right, of course. He unwrapped the stuff Chan had gotten at the store. Granddad and Grandma Chandler had given him a compass, a nice one in a stainless steel casing.

Grandma Lincoln had made Linc a pair of navy gabardine trousers that were finished except for the hems. "I was unsure just how much you'd grown, so if you'll try them on later, I'll put the hem in before I start back home."

Polly's mother had moved to New Orleans and set up her shop just after Polly had gotten married. She'd probably stay a few days after the Chandlers had left for their golf tournament just to visit her daughter.

"No need to do that, Mother. After all, you're on your vacation," Polly said. "I can do it when everyone is gone."

"I like to finish what I start, Polly," Grandma said. "Professional pride, I suppose."

"I guess I'm not as good as you, Mother, but I feel I do an adequate job of sewing," Linc's mother said, hurt dripping from her words. "Don't let Grandma get too close a look at my gift, Linc. She'll see all the flaws." She handed Linc a large package, then leaned back in her chair, sulking.

Polly had made him a lined jacket in his school colors. "It's beautiful, Mom, just what I wanted."

"Then you don't like the trousers?" Grandma asked.

"I love the trousers, Grandma. They're perfect." He thought he knew how diplomats must feel, being buffeted between opposing sides.

"Well, all right."

Linc stacked his presents together and slid them back under the tree. Except for the hunting gear, it was not his worst Christmas ever.

With that necessary formality over, Chan jumped up and headed for the den. "Kick-off, Dad, Linc." The television set popped on for the back-to-back football games, which would run for the rest of the day. Linc wasn't really interested in watching teams that weren't from their area and had no hometown heroes on them, but he hung around for as long as he could in what his mother called the "male bonding."

"Gee, I hate to leave," Linc finally said, "but I'm supposed to go over to Ginger's for our present exchange."

"Did you see that play?" Chan exclaimed. "What a tackle." He reached into his pocket, barely taking his eyes off the screen. "Here, Linc, catch." He threw the keys to the jeep toward him.

"Gee, thanks, Dad," Linc said. "I'll be careful with it." But Chan was already deeply absorbed in the game. Linc couldn't help but wonder at Chan's mood. He seemed really relaxed and happy, for a change. And generous. Was it because he was going hunting tomorrow? Or was it because he was going hunting with his only son?

The last of the Rawlingses' guests were just leaving when Linc got there. Ginger swept him into the house and pointed above her head. "Mistletoe, Linc."

He encircled her slim shoulders and planted a solid kiss on her until he heard a throat clearing.

"Merry Christmas, Linc." It was Mr. Rawlings. "You didn't stay long at the cast party last night."

"No, sir," Linc said, pulling back guiltily. "I'd promised my folks I'd get my sister home as early as possible. They're still pretty strict with her."

Mr. Rawlings looked at Ginger. "Wise decision. No need to let go of the kite string too soon."

Linc wanted to tell Mr. Rawlings that the tighter you held to a kite string, the less likely it was ever to fly. But that seemed an argument worth saving for his own parents.

"Well, I'll leave you two to your gift exchanges and visiting. The Honolulu ball game will be coming on soon. Odd to think of it so early there, isn't it?" He looked at Linc long and hard before finally leaving the room.

"Why do I get the feeling that he thinks I'm some sort of pervert?" Linc whispered into Ginger's ear once her father was gone.

Ginger giggled. "Aren't you?" She led him to the sofa, which glowed prettily in the reflection of the multicolored lights on the tree. "Sit here. I'll get us some wassail. It's still hot in the teapot."

Ginger returned with steaming cups smelling of apple and spices. Linc took a sip, then set his cup on the coffee table. He reached into his pocket and pulled out the small package. "Merry Christmas," he said. "I guess this isn't much, but . . ."

"Good things come in small packages, Linc, and I'll love whatever you've given me." With her slender fingers, Ginger flicked off the ribbon and tore the cellophane tape. Linc watched as she lifted the lid and pulled back the cotton. "Oh, Linc, barrettes. And they're engraved. They're lovely."

Ginger slipped a barrette onto each side of her hair, and they glistened in the reflection of the lights. "I'll treasure them." She went over to the tree and pulled a large box from under it. It was a set of pastels, some charcoal pencils, and some linen-textured drawing paper. "You've used up so much on me, I thought I should get you some for Christmas.

"I'll bet you didn't even notice," Ginger continued, pointing toward the fireplace mantle. "Doesn't it look great there? Mother gave me the frame for Christmas, and I just couldn't wait to use it for the sketch."

She had placed the *Nutcracker* sketch in a silver frame. It looked pretty good, nestled among the boughs of holly and pine. Of course, Linc thought, such a setting might make a feed-store calendar look good, too. "And I saved you some posters and programs. I'm so proud of you, Linc."

"I'll take these along on the trip," he said. "That way, maybe it won't be a loss." He glanced back at the sketch. "Ginger, isn't it a letdown, working so hard for so long on the ballet, then having it be over in a flash?"

Ginger took his hand and squeezed it gently. "In a way, but then I look forward to the next challenge. That's really what it's all about."

"But isn't your dancing life going to be kind of short? I mean, you won't be able to do it forever." Immediately he was sorry he'd said that.

Ginger gazed at the tree lights as she spoke. "I just have to dance. I don't know, maybe I can teach or choreograph later, or maybe I'll just drive my own kids crazy, insisting that they take classes."

Linc looked away.

"I know you're thinking about the trip, Linc. Try to look at it positively. Maybe you and your dad will become closer on the trip. You've always wanted that, haven't you?"

"Yeah, but *his* way? No way! It's just like when Mom and Dad are around their parents. They might as well be five years old again. And it's the same with me and Dad."

"I guess it's up to you, the enlightened one, to break the cycle. Just remember this when you have kids of your own." Ginger patted his cheek.

"I'll think about you every second you're gone," Ginger promised.

"You, too," he said, pulling her close.

12

THE sun wasn't yet up, and fog curled from the ground, which was still wet. Although Polly was awake, Chan insisted that they eat breakfast on the road. "It always tastes better on the road," he said.

Linc waved to his mother as they drove out. She looked tired and even a little relieved. Was it because she really believed he and his dad were making progress in their relationship? Or was it simply because Chan would be gone a whole week?

"Are Grandma and Mom going to be okay, you think?" Linc wanted to know.

"Probably," Chan replied. "They can use the time alone. There's still a lot they need to find out about each other."

Linc looked at his father, surprised. Maybe there was something beyond all that football jumble.

As they pulled from the drive, Linc glanced up to see the curtain in the den window open. Betty's face appeared at the window. She held up her hand to show crossed fingers. Linc acknowledged her good wishes with a nod. Silently, he wished well for Betty, too. After all, she was stuck with Polly and Grandma.

They had been on the road for about an hour when Chan

pulled into a roadside diner where several pickup trucks and a car were parked. Inside it was warm and humid and smelled of grease. A large-mouthed waitress who reminded Linc of a television sitcom he'd seen once sashayed between the tables, making small talk with a scattering of men in western hats or deerstalkers, most of whom were obviously hunters on the way to their own kills.

"Why, hi, there," she greeted Chan and Linc. "I remember that handsome face from last year, hon. Why, you done got yourself a partner! He's so little, I'd have to throw him back." She threw back her head and laughed before handing them menus.

Chan slung his arm around the woman's hips and drew her closer. "This here's my son, sweetheart. He's going on his first hunting trip with his old dad."

She patted Chan on the back, laughing. "My goodness, a *virgin* hunter! But he can't be your boy, you're so young!"

Chan grinned broadly and patted the waitress on the rear, obviously enjoying the flattery a lot. "Bring us your strongest, hottest coffee for now, sugar, and we'll make up our minds about what to order in the meanwhile." His accent was getting thicker by the minute.

Linc had a real urge to punch his father in the nose. Why was he acting like such a fool, and why didn't that woman have enough pride to dump a pot of hot coffee on him? Clamping his teeth, he studied the menu intently and didn't look up when the waitress returned with the coffee.

"Orange juice, two eggs over easy, sausage, and whole wheat toast, please," Linc told the waitress.

"How 'bout you, hon?" the waitress asked.

"Make that OJ, *three* eggs scrambled, sausage, and plenty of butter on the toast, okay, sugar?"

When Linc was sure she'd left, he excused himself and

went to the restroom. It was dingy looking because of a light bulb with too little wattage and dark walls and linoleum. He leaned over the sink and dashed cold water on his face. His father was being a real jerk. Why? Was he trying to prove something? At least he had seemed proud of Linc when he introduced him.

But freezing outdoors in the cold morning mist or maybe even sleet this time of year, hunched in a bedroll or shivering behind bushes, was his dad's love, not Linc's. And the farther from home they got, the more treacherous the weather became. Even the flaps tightly snapped on the jeep's sides failed to shut out the bone-numbing cold. Linc's breath made little puffs of fog as he spoke. "How much farther is it, Dad? Gee, what I wouldn't give for a hot, steamy bath right now."

His father laughed. "Yeah, great, isn't it? Nothing but us and nature. We'll spend the night in a motel in Odessa, and that's the last of civilization we'll see for a week. Ah, this is the life, right, son?" His face seemed flushed and a little swollen, probably from excitement, Linc figured.

"Yeah, Dad, right." The miserable life. The life he never wanted to see after this week.

The distance between towns grew, and there were long stretches of mesquite and scrub brush. Linc noticed a scattering of cactus and posted, fenced lands that were fairly well forested. Although the sun was hidden by a thick layer of gray, the area was bright in its beauty.

"Bleak, huh?" Chan said.

"Yeah, Dad, bleak." They were nothing alike. They never would be. Why was he even trying to find common ground?

The jeep sped along the narrow highway, having to contend with little traffic. Only when they neared towns sprinkled sparsely along the way did they run into more than a half dozen cars at a time.

It was already dark when they pulled up in front of a motel in Odessa. "It says no vacancy, Dad," Linc said, pointing to the neon sign at the edge of the parking lot.

"That's for jerks with no foresight! We've got reservations," Chan said, sliding out of the car. "Stay here with the gear, and I'll get us registered. I'll leave the motor running so you'll have heat."

Lord, had the heater been on all that time? It mustn't be very effective, or else the temperature was lower than he even dared imagine. Crossing his arms above his chest, Linc slapped his upper arms, testing for feeling. They were still there.

Chan bounced back into the jeep and said, "We're in 173, around back."

He wheeled the jeep around to the back, down the long line of look-alike doors and beyond campers, pickups, and cars of every description. "Help me get this gear inside," he said.

Linc didn't argue. All he could think about was getting indoors. He threw his backpack over his shoulders and snatched the rifles and ammunition, scurrying for the door, which Chan had thrown open.

It was pitch dark inside, and cold. The heat wasn't on. Still, it was better than being outside. Linc found the switch and flipped on the lights. The room was small and a dirty gray with twin beds, each topped with a red, orange, and yellow blanket of imitation Indian design. He quickly located the heat switch on the unit beneath the window and turned it on. A rush of warm air came out, and Linc paused to enjoy it before Chan yelled from outside to get the rest of the stuff and be quick about it.

They'd no sooner thrown their gear into a corner of the small, cramped room than Chan said, "Okay, let's get a bite to eat next door."

"Outside again?" Linc asked.

"I hope you weren't expecting room service in a place like this," Chan said, laughing.

Linc sighed. "There's always hope."

Since they were situated well at the back of the motel, they jumped into the jeep and drove the short distance to the restaurant. Condensation trickled down the windows, and Linc bounded into the restaurant eagerly. "I'm starving," he confessed.

"Eat heartily," Chan said. "Except for a quick breakfast, this is the last meal you'll get for a while that somebody else cooked."

Linc had chicken-fried steak, a baked potato, lima beans, and fresh-baked rolls.

"Gimme the biggest porterhouse steak, a heaping order of french fried potatoes, and don't bother with any sprigs of green junk, okay, honey?" Chan told the waitress. "And keep the Pearl coming." He rubbed his stomach. "I'm starved, too. I'm so empty it hurts."

Linc squinted at him. "You look kinda flushed, Dad. Are you all right?"

"I'm fine. It's just the lighting in here, that's all."

It was late, near closing, and most of the customers had cleared out. Linc ate, then leaned on the table, studying the remaining people while his father devoured a bowl of peach cobbler with a scoop of vanilla ice cream on top.

A couple of truckers were engaged in deep conversation with the waitress, who didn't seem much older than Linc. She fussed with the salt and pepper shakers near her as she spoke with them. The girl was definitely uncomfortable.

89

She probably didn't want to be there any more than he did.

Chan rubbed his chest. "This place doesn't serve food cooked any better than your mother's." He fished through his shirt pocket and pulled out a couple of antacid tablets.

"I don't see anything wrong with the food. Are you sure you're okay, Dad?" Linc wanted to know.

"I'm fine! It was just lousy food, okay?"

They went back to the motel room and heard a party going on next door. From the boisterous conversation spilling into the Chandlers' room, Linc figured it was a group of hunters either going or coming. They spun tales of one encounter after another with deer, game wardens, and women, punctuating each tale with uproarious laughter well into the night.

Linc tossed and turned in the bed. It wasn't very comfortable, and even when he covered his ears with the pillow, the noise still came through.

In the other bed, his father alternated tossing and turning with fits of snoring, until he gagged and started coughing. Then he continued tossing and turning.

Chan seemed fit enough the next morning, though. He was obviously spurred on by his desire to get to the leased land as soon as possible.

Linc put on a set of thermal underwear, a flannel shirt, and the thickest jeans he'd brought. He unpacked his heavy lined jacket.

When they arrived for breakfast at the same restaurant, a pickup truck was parked near the door. The bodies of two stags were tied to the front fenders, their eyes staring lifelessly skyward.

Linc hesitantly reached out to touch one. The fur was laced with dew and stiff. He drew back his hand, staring.

"A beaut, huh?" his father said.

90

"It was once," Linc mumbled. His stomach churned and rejected breakfast, and Linc finally settled for a cup of hot chocolate.

Afterward, they repacked their gear in the jeep, checked out of the motel, and set out once more. The sun had no better luck piercing the clouds than it had the day before. It began to sprinkle about ten-thirty.

Linc could tell this was going to be a corker of a trip. His feet were numb in his boots, and his nose felt cold and drippy. If he was getting a cold . . .

About midday, the jeep pulled to the side of the road and Chan leaned toward Linc to read a hand-painted sign staked in the dirt shoulder. "Does that say Sutters Ranch?"

"Yeah, Dad," Linc said, squinting through the sleet. "The arrow points down this rock road. And it says Private Road."

Rocks spun out from the jeep wheels as it maneuvered around potholes and bumped along the narrow road that seemed endless to Linc.

"How far off the road *is* the ranch?" Linc wanted to know.

"The ranch house is on the main road, a couple of miles," Chan said. "We're on the ranch now. We're just going to the part leased by Mr. M."

Linc had no idea that so much land could belong to anyone. There wasn't a house or barn in sight.

Chan finally pulled the jeep up onto the dirt shoulder of the road next to a fence that said AREA SEVEN. POSTED. KEEP OUT. NO HUNTING, EXCEPT WITH PERMISSION OF THE OWNER. A crude gate wide enough for a car was padlocked.

"Hop out and open her up," Chan said, handing a key on a chain to Linc. "We'll go inside as far as we can maneuver the jeep, set up base camp there, and be free to fan out in any direction inside the fence perimeters."

Linc took the key and unlocked the gate as swiftly as he could. The cold made it difficult to hold the key. He couldn't imagine why he hadn't unpacked his gloves that morning. He swung the gate open, allowing Chan to drive through before swinging it shut again.

"Shall I lock it back?" Linc shouted, but either Chan was too distracted, or he couldn't hear above the motor.

Linc yelled several times before Chan opened the jeep flap. "Huh?"

Linc repeated his question.

"Yeah! We've got it all to ourselves."

Linc stood, staring around him. It was as if they were shut off from the whole world. Alone together. He could tell this was going to be a real fun time.

13

DESPITE his seatbelt, Linc felt as if he had to hold onto the dash to keep himself from being bounced right out of the jeep as Chan wove it between the mesquite trees and over the underbrush.

"What's that?" Linc yelled above the noise of the struggling engine. It was a lump of white stuff.

"That's a salt lick," Chan yelled back. "The deer will come for a special treat all year and get used to it. They'll stay in the area."

It wasn't sport hunting, Linc thought, but murder. "It doesn't seem right," he said as Chan pulled to a stop and shut off the engine.

"What doesn't?"

"To get them used to some kind of lure. I rank that with cops hiding behind signboards."

Chan laughed. "You'd be surprised! Deer always seem to know when hunting season is on. You can come here the day before, and they'll look you right in the eye if you walk up to them. The next day, when season starts, they all disappear. Somehow they know."

Linc looked away from his father. What was to know?

They heard the horrible sound of gunfire ringing through-out their quiet peaceful home, and then one by one they didn't show up. Did they grieve over loved ones like humans? Linc wondered. He remembered reading about a gorilla that lost its kitten and grieved. Maybe all creatures did. He felt weird out here.

They came to a clearing and could go no farther. The area showed evidence of old camps. Mesquite branches were stacked at one side, as if waiting to be used for firewood. A narrow stream snaked through the area.

In the distance, rifle shots rang out. Poor creatures. Run, hide, Linc thought. There are even more of us now than before.

"Come on, let's get this tent set up and the gear stowed and a fire going. Then we'll eat something."

Although the sleet had stopped, Linc hugged himself, trying to generate a little warmth. "Does it have to be in that order?" he asked. "Can't we start a fire first?"

"It'd be hard to set up the tent in the dark, so we'll do that first," Chan told him.

When they'd set up the tent and installed the bedrolls, Chan said, "Be careful picking up those pieces of mesquite. They've been stacked a long time, and snakes may have chosen them as a place to hibernate."

"Oh, great," Linc muttered. "Just great. Hours from civilization, and we're living with snakes?"

"It's too cold for them to stir," Chan said. "But I don't know how they'd react if they were disturbed from hibernation. Maybe they're in too deep a sleep to notice."

"They'd notice," Linc said. "It'd be my luck that they'd notice." Gingerly, poking each branch first, watching for any movement around it, Linc gathered enough of the mesquite limbs to start a fire. Soon the sweet smell reminded him of the restaurants back home that specialized in mesquite cooking.

The food didn't remind him of the restaurants, though. They heated up cans of pork and beans and ate cold beef jerky. "It'll make us lean and mean," Chan said. "We'll be ready for the kill."

That staved off starvation. Later Linc opened a couple of cans of chili and hung them above the fire to simmer. By the time they had eaten their real meal, it was dark. Luckily for the deer, it was illegal to hunt them at night, or Linc was sure that Chan would've insisted on hunting right then.

The temperature had fallen quickly, and the chill settled in every joint in Linc's body. He silently wished that he were at least back in the motel, noisy neighbors and all. Almost anything would be better than this. He paused and looked around him. Everything seemed to be varying shades of silver and gray.

But the gnarled tree limbs and the tangle of dried-out underbrush had almost poetic form. Stark as it might seem at first glance, there was real beauty there. Linc was tempted to whip out his sketch pad. Tempted, yes, but he wasn't crazy. The sketch pad would have to wait until another time, a time when his father was distracted.

Quick, yelping noises followed by eerie howling sounded in the distance to Linc's left. "I hear a dog," he said. "We must be closer to the ranch house than you thought." There was an answering cry to Linc's right.

"That's no dog. That's coyote," Chan said reaching into his duffle bag and taking out a beer. "It's always hunting season for those beasts." He popped the can open, and foam oozed up and over the side. "Ah," he said, "almost as cold as if it'd come from the fridge."

"Dad, do you have to?" Linc said. Nothing scared him more than alcohol and guns mixed together.

"Aw," Chan said in an almost boyish tone, "you sound like my father. Relax."

The coyotes continued their howling and yipping, each time seeming to get closer together somewhere in the distance. Linc peered beyond the fire into the darkness, wondering how many there were in the pack. Their yips and howls had definite patterns, like a real conversation. Like a night song.

Chan stood up. "I'll keep the rifle close tonight, just in case. But I don't think they'll come near the camp. Be sure that all the food is closed up so as not to attract them. If you see one, shoot it. You'll be doing the rancher a favor."

Linc got a couple more mesquite limbs and put them on the fire.

Chan had paused at the tent entrance to look back at Linc. "Aren't you coming to bed, son?"

"Not just yet. I want to stay up a while." His clothes were hot to the touch, but he realized that wouldn't last long after he left the fire. At least the sleet had finally stopped, although a heavy mist had settled in.

"We'll get an early start tomorrow. Don't stay up too late. And don't let those coyotes make you nervous. They won't come into camp."

"I'm not nervous about them. I'll be in soon."

"Linc?"

"Yeah, Dad?"

"I'm glad you came."

"Me, too, Dad." In a way, he was. There had been no cross words between them. Maybe this really was a chance to get closer.

Chan shut the tent flap and was snoring within minutes.

After a while, Linc tried, but he finally decided that he was not intended for sleeping on the ground in a downy bedroll.

Linc finally slipped from the tent and restoked the fire. The moon had risen and illuminated the misty fog. The silhouette of a gnarled tree near the stream captured Linc's attention. Slipping the pencils and sketch pad Ginger had given him from his backpack, Linc made bold strokes across the first page, outlining the skeletal shape of the tree and frozen stream. His hands glided over the page swiftly, and he became unaware of the cold that had so plagued him only minutes before.

A movement caught his attention as something large stirred at the stream. Linc blinked. A stag, its horns an intricate tangle of symmetrical design, glided into view. With one slender hoof, it cracked the thin layer of ice on the narrow stream and straddled the water, drinking. Then it lifted its head and stared directly at Linc. Its fur glistened in the firelight, and its dark eyes reflected the flickering flame. Every muscle was taut; it was ready to run in an instant.

Linc was suddenly aware of an ache in his chest. He had been holding his breath and gradually let it go. That small sound was enough to spook the stag, and it took off, leaping over the underbrush with Ginger-like grace.

What a sight! It had been worth the whole ugly trip to see that beautiful stag standing there looking at him.

The sun wasn't even up when Linc was roughly roused from an uneasy sleep.

"Dammit, Linc!" It was Chan at the tent entrance. "I bring you out here in hopes that you'll act like a man and you bring that sissy junk even here. Dammit. I'd hoped it would be different out here, away from everything."

"So had I, Dad," Linc muttered. "So had I."

"Java's already boiled," Chan said. "Bacon's cooking. Shake a leg."

It seemed strange to Linc that his father was cooking. At home, he would have starved before entering the kitchen for more than his own can of beer, and he wouldn't have done that if he could get his wife or one of his kids to get it for him. Some guys who wouldn't cook in the kitchen would barbecue. But "Chan the Man" didn't even do that.

Linc figured the worst thing about camping was relieving himself in the frigid open air. It was humiliating and seemed to dare the elements.

Actually, the coffee might have been the worst thing. Although he didn't like coffee under the best of circumstances, he thought he wouldn't mind having anything hot. But it tasted like mud. "Why so early, Dad? We've got the whole week, and you said yourself the limit is two bucks."

"Four. Two for each of us," Chan said. His voice held an edge of anger, and puffs of fog formed as he spoke.

Linc imagined that it was steam. "You don't expect me to kill two deer, uh, my first season, do you?"

"Doesn't matter who bags them. The warden, assuming he even sees us, just makes sure there aren't more deer than hunting licenses in a group. Now stow the food, and let's get started."

"But it's still dark," Linc argued. "Isn't it against the law to hunt before daylight?"

"There's no law that says we can't stalk. I spotted some hoofprints over by the stream. Brazen suckers come right up by us to drink. We can follow those."

Oh, no, Linc thought. How could he stalk that stag?

"But, Dad," Linc said, trying his last idea, "you still haven't shown me how to fire the rifle. I'm not sure I can do it under pressure without practicing."

"Cripes," Chan said. "You just look through the sight and pull the trigger, Linc! Now, let's get going. The first light's already here."

"Are you all right, Dad? You look—I don't know, you look different, sort of flushed and swollen faced. When did you have your blood pressure checked?"

"I'm healthy as a horse. And strong as one, too. I'm just aggravated with you, that's all. You carry the gear, Linc. My arm is out of whack this morning. I guess I must've slept on it or something."

"What do you mean, out of whack, Dad? Maybe we'd better stay in camp. Or find a doctor or something."

"Maybe we'd better get started," Chan growled.

Reluctantly, Linc grabbed the rifles by their leather straps and slung them across his back, barrel up, following Chan through the brush.

"For Pete's sake, Linc," Chan whispered. "A herd of elephants would make less noise. Don't you know how to walk quietly?"

He did, for that matter, but Linc had hoped that if he made enough noise, he'd drive away whatever deer were in the area.

14

WHEN they finally left camp, the sun was doing a pretty good job of shining through low clouds, although it didn't add much warmth.

Chan paused and rubbed his left arm. He was breathing pretty hard, although they were going at a slow pace. "Let's sit a minute," he said. "I don't know why the devil Mr. M. didn't set up deer blinds, anyway. Slogging around out here, with no idea where we're going. It's stupid."

"Deer blinds? What are those?" Linc asked.

"A shelter where we stay warm and deer can't see us. Don't you know anything?" Frosty sweat beads had formed above Chan's face, and his eyes looked a bit red rimmed and frantic.

"Dad, are you sure you're all right?"

"Yes." Chan rubbed his chest and arm. More quietly he said, "Yes, I'm all right. I guess my cooking didn't agree with me. Let's move it." He stood, weaving a moment until he found his balance.

Linc figured it was probably all that weight his dad had put on. Granddad was right. Chan should be working out and cutting down on some of the fat stuff.

"Get the rifles, Linc, for crying out loud!"

"Oh, sorry," Linc apologized, slightly amused. It had been unintentional, but leaving them behind would've been a good idea, had his dad not noticed.

A low limb on a bush had been snapped off, it seemed recently. There was a tuft of honey-colored fur clinging to the limb. "This way," Chan said.

Suddenly Chan put up an arm to stop Linc. He shoved him downward, signaling for him to be quiet. Linc peered beyond Chan to see a beautiful stag—he was sure it was the same one—standing quite still, listening for sound. Oh, run, please run. Don't stand there and be shot down for Chan's ego!

"Gimme the rifle," Chan whispered.

When Linc hesitated, Chan grimaced and said as quietly as he could, "Gimme the rifle, and I mean *now*."

Reluctantly, Linc handed Chan a rifle. "Not yours, mine," Chan said. "And hurry up."

Linc handed Chan the other rifle. He couldn't tell the difference between them.

The stag turned toward them and sniffed suspiciously, but still didn't move. Linc fought the urge to stand up and shout, to drive the stag away. He hated himself for his lack of courage.

"Gimme the ammo," Chan whispered. "Be quick about it."

Linc raised an eyebrow. "Ammo?" He burst into rolling laughter. If he'd planned it any better, it couldn't have worked out so well. He held his sides and whooped.

The stag turned on its heels and disappeared behind some brush.

"Dammit, Linc, you didn't bring the ammo? Of all the dumb—"

Linc brushed away the tears that had gathered in his eyes. "You just said bring the guns."

"Rifles. I never say guns when I mean rifles."

"Okay, but I was sure—"

"I said gear. Gear! I said get the gear. That means rifles, ammo, anything else that a hunter needs, dammit! I could've had that stag, too!"

"This is my first trip, Dad. I didn't—"

"You're as dumb as your mother."

Linc suddenly felt hot inside his down jacket. "Hold it! You can call me anything you want—and usually do. You can slug me if you think you can. But you can't talk about my mother that way. She's not dumb!" The only thing dumb she ever did was marry him.

"Don't talk to me like that, boy! Don't you ever raise your voice to me like that."

"Don't you ever call my mother dumb. You apologize! I mean it."

Linc grabbed the rifles and stalked off.

"Where are you going?" Chan demanded.

"I'm going back to camp."

"You'll get lost, wandering around by yourself like that. Wait for me."

"I've got a compass, remember?" Linc didn't look back to see if his father was following. In a way he hoped Chan would get lost and never show up. The family would be a lot better off without him.

Linc had started a campfire, and as he got warmer, he began to worry about Chan. He glanced at his watch. What if his father really was wandering around out there, lost? Of course he didn't believe they'd be better off without Chan. He heated some stew. Chan would be hungry when he got back—if he got back.

By the time the stew was bubbling, Chan made it into camp and slumped onto a folding stool, breathing heavily. He looked flushed in the face, yet pale around the lips, and Linc was immediately sorry that he'd left him behind.

Linc didn't say anything. Instead, he stirred the stew without looking up, until Chan finally spoke. "I—I didn't mean what I said about your mother."

Linc still didn't look up.

"She is not dumb. Polly is a clever woman and she makes a good wife and mother."

"What about me?" Linc said. "I don't hear you saying I'm not dumb, that I make a good son."

"I was angry. I should've instructed you better about your rifle."

Linc dipped some stew into a tin plate and handed it to Chan.

"I thought anybody would know to take along ammo."

Anybody but his dumb son, his sissy son, the son he never wanted.

"We'll eat, rest a while. Then I'll help you with your rifle. You can practice. Then we'll go out."

Linc dipped the ladle into the stew and poured himself some. He pulled his stool closer to the fire and sat down, concentrating on eating.

"But you should have known better," Chan muttered between bites.

Linc took a big bite and chewed deliberately, staring into the fire.

"Well, dammit, you should've!" Chan said. "I bring you out here in hopes of turning you into a man. I even apologize, and you sit there sulking like a baby. Say something."

Linc slammed his plate down on the ground. Some stew oozed over the rim and spilled into the fire with a sizzle.

"You've said a lot of stuff, but no, you didn't apologize. Not really. I never heard you say that you're sorry. And as for being a man, it doesn't take killing a deer or screwing everything in skirts to make me a man. It doesn't even take muscles or football. It's what's in here." Linc touched his head. "And here." He touched his heart. Then Linc felt his skin grow hot as he realized what he'd said—and that he finally believed it. If only he could convince his father. Or did he really have to? Maybe it was enough that *he* knew.

The spot on Chan's forehead throbbed, and his jawline squared. "Set up the stew cans on that stump over there."

Linc set the cans as he'd been told and returned to the campfire.

The rifle clicked as Chan pulled it open and inserted shells into the chambers. "This is the way you load." He snapped it shut. "Load your rifle."

Grim-faced, Linc did it.

"Now set your sight on the can on the right. Just a little low. The tendency is to pull up slightly when you fire. Aim and fire."

Linc squeezed the trigger, and the stock pounded into his shoulder, nearly knocking him to the ground. The can was still there, untouched.

"Use your chest to steady your arm, and try again."

Again Linc fired, and this time he hit the stump.

"Close enough," Chan said. "A deer's a big target. If you can aim at the can and hit the stump, you'll do all right. You'll be able to slow it down enough to catch up and finish the job." He took a deep breath. "I'm going to let my lunch settle awhile. Then we'll go out again." Sluggishly, he went into the tent.

Linc had known all along that they'd gotten up too early. It was stupid to get up so early and then have a long day of boredom. He cleaned the plates and the stew pot in water from the brook, which he heated. When he'd finished, he instinctively reached for his sketch pad and pencil. It didn't matter if his father saw him now.

When Chan came out of the tent later, he looked better. "Get the gear—the rifles and the ammo, Linc. Let's see if we can't pick up the trail of that stag."

Lord, Linc thought as he gathered the pouch of ammo and picked up the rifles, is it still only the first day out here? He felt as if he'd aged a lifetime.

He trudged behind Chan, who got more and more agitated as they circled and retraced their steps and ran into their own trail.

"This lease is a gyp," Chan grumbled. "No deer on the stupid property. I'm beginning to think that stag was just an illusion."

They crossed the stream a couple of times, doubling back and turning this way and that until they finally came to a barbed wire fence.

"That's the end of the property Mr. M. leased, I guess," Linc said gratefully. Now maybe they'd give up and return to camp.

"It's a ripoff. He probably feeds the deer over there and keeps them for himself," Chan said.

"Yeah, well, I guess we can go."

Chan pulled a tuft of brown fur off a barb. "Deer must've cut too low going over the fence. I knew it. Darn deer are all over there, not on this stupid lease."

"Well," Linc said lightly, "that's the luck of the hunt. Let's—"

"If the deer won't come to us, we'll go to them," Chan muttered as he gingerly stretched the barbed wire. "It all belongs to the same rancher, anyway. He won't care."

"Dad!" Linc yelled. "Dad, look at the sign on the fence. It says, Private property. Trespassers will be prosecuted."

"So's this property. But that doesn't mean anything. We've got a right to be here."

"But not there, Dad. There's a warning, too. It says it's dangerous!" Linc read the sign aloud. "Posted. Danger. Coyote cyanide traps."

But Chan was already on the other side of the fence. "These are hoofprints, not coyote prints. Come on."

"But, Dad."

"I said, come on—unless you're scared," Chan challenged. "You going to be a crybaby all your life?"

Linc stood there, staring at the fence. He'd heard about coyote cyanide traps. They'd been outlawed once, but some nothing politician had gotten them made legal again, as long as they were labeled and warnings were posted. They were explosives buried in pipes in the ground. One touch and cyanide-coated missiles shot in every direction. It was a painful and sure death, and it didn't discriminate among coyote, cow, or human. Either his father was crazy, or he really was sure that the sign was meaningless.

Linc took a deep breath and leaned the rifles against the fence post. He watched his father trudge deeper into the forbidden property. This could be dangerous and stupid. But his father was an experienced hunter. "Just a minute, Dad," he shouted. "I'm coming."

15

LINC couldn't help but feel that Chan was getting them into trouble, big trouble. But he couldn't have stayed on the other side of the fence, no matter what the danger, and let his dad go wandering about in the state he was in.

At least the sign said that the cyanide traps were labeled. So all they had to do was look for signs and avoid those areas, just in case.

Heavy gray clouds had obliterated the sun, and a chill clung to the air. The rifles and ammo bag Linc carried grew heavier with each step.

"I can't find the hoofprints on this side," Chan said. "He had to pass somewhere around here."

"He probably didn't come this way then," Linc answered. "He probably just rubbed up against the barbs on the other side. You know, the way cows do to scratch an itch, or something."

"He came this way, I'm sure of it," Chan insisted. "That was belly hair, as if he were leaping and didn't jump high enough."

"You said they were smart," Linc argued. "He's probably on the other side, laughing at us."

Chan rubbed his arm, then his chest. "I didn't say they were that smart. C'mon, this way."

Linc could feel his armpits getting damp. Maybe he should take off his jacket. No, that was stupid. It was cold. The camp thermometer had read 30° that morning.

Chan was bounding ahead now with renewed enthusiasm. "Found some prints. This way. Stay with me, son. Right behind me." He pointed to his right. There was a crude sign about ankle height and the size of a piece of bread, with a faded red skull and crossbones on it. The deadly pipe was barely visible above the ground. There *were* cyanide traps there. Now they both knew it.

Why would anybody want to kill coyotes? Linc wondered as he stumbled along behind his father. They were the true ecological answer to trimming herds of deer and killing off rodents and the like. He'd read all about them for a nature report in school in the ninth grade.

For his report, he'd clipped a newspaper article about a farmer on the outskirts of town who had killed off the wolves and coyotes in the area. The unimpeded rodents had then devoured his corn and oat crops. Too late, he'd realized the importance of the coyotes in the ecological system. And they hunted the sick and weak among larger animals. Besides, Linc thought, remembering last evening, their night song was so beautiful.

They passed another cyanide trap and, not far away, a jackrabbit's carcass. The unfortunate rabbit had probably stumbled into the gun while foraging for food. And whatever foraged on the jackrabbit now would die from eating the cyanide-tainted meat, and on and on. That included the eagles or any other endangered species that might stray into the area.

Chan had slowed his pace and was breathing hard. The

potential danger must be getting to him, too, Linc figured. "Dad, please, let's go back to our lease."

"I want that stag. I saw him. He's mine." Chan's face was drenched in sweat, despite the temperature.

"I don't feel right about this," Linc said. "I'm going back." He hoped his father would follow him, if for no other reason than to bawl him out. Anything to get back to the camp.

Linc did a 180-degree spin. Which way was the camp? They'd lost sight of the fence. He felt for his compass. It wasn't there. He must've left it back at camp. Dad was right, he had no sense about camping at all.

"Linc, no!" Chan's voice rose an octave.

Linc looked back just in time to see Chan making a dive for him.

He *is* crazy! Linc thought as he braced himself. Chan's full weight hit Linc, lifting him up and off the ground. Chan knocked him three, maybe even five feet from where he'd been. It was a real "Chan the Man" tackle. They both hit the ground hard and lay there, gasping.

"Wh-what's the matter with you?" Linc demanded. "Have you lost it?" He took gasping breaths, trying to refill his lungs.

"G-gun," Chan stammered. "Cy-nide." He nodded to where Linc's next step would've been. Jutting ever so slightly from the ground was a cyanide pellet gun. The warning sign lay face down by it.

"I-I would've bought it. Th-thanks, Dad. You saved my life."

At great risk to himself, Linc realized. Had Chan missed the tackle, or had they landed on the gun instead of away from it, they'd have both died. Linc shuddered, thinking that they might have been the next carrion left behind.

Chan moaned and grasped his chest. His breath was coming in uneven gulps. He clutched at his jacket, loosening it, rolling his eyes.

Dear god, had the gun gone off, after all? Linc didn't remember an explosive sound. But maybe he hadn't heard it? "What is it, Dad? What?"

Frantically, Linc inspected his father's clothing. There'd be tears, entry holes in his clothes, wouldn't there? It couldn't have been the gun.

"Chest hu-hurts," Chan said. "Left arm h-hurts. D-d-don't let me die, Linc." Tears welled in Chan's eyes.

It hit Linc like a rock between the eyes. Chan was having a heart attack! "Help!" Linc yelled. "Somebody help! Help us, please!"

There was nobody to hear. Should he signal with a rifle? No, that would be stupid. There was rifle fire everywhere. He'd have to walk Chan out of there. No, he couldn't do that. He'd kill him for sure. Chan had to stay still, calm.

"Don't worry, Dad. Don't worry. Breathe in through your nose, deep breaths, out through your mouth. That's it. In, out, in, out. Calm. Stay calm. I'm going to get you help."

The clouds were too thick for Linc to see the sun. He couldn't judge direction, and didn't know how far they were in. He would make a stretcher, that was it, pull him out. With what? "Don't worry, Dad. I'm going to get you out of here. Get you to a doctor. Don't worry."

There was no hatchet to cut mesquite limbs. He should have brought the hatchet. He tore at the mesquite with his bare hands, bending it, twisting it this way and that, but it failed to snap. He needed poles, something stiff.

Rifles! The rifles would make the frame. The damn rifles would be good for something.

What was he going to use for a sling? His jacket? It wasn't

strong enough, but he could piece it together with his flannel shirt. Yes, it had to work. Could he use Chan's jacket? No, his father had to stay warm, warm and still.

As swiftly as he could, Linc tied together the sleeves of his jacket and shirt. He was cold, shaking like a leaf. His long johns would have to keep him warm, that was all there was to it. Linc tied the rifle butts together into a V-shape, then stretched the shirt between the rifles. The sling was too small. What could he do? "Hold on, Dad. Everything's gonna be all right."

He unhooked an end of each rifle strap and used one to make a slat, extending the sling. The other he would use as a pull. Now he had to get Chan onto the sling. "Don't worry, Dad. Everything's gonna be okay."

He had to strap Chan on somehow. But how? The ammo bag; it had long straps. He turned the bag upside down, and ammunition scattered across the ground like brass insects.

Grabbing Chan under the arms Linc lifted him slightly, sliding the makeshift sling under him. He buttoned the jacket around Chan's shoulders and fastened the strap. He needed more. Of course! Chan's belt, and his own. He hastily slipped those off and wrapped them around Chan, buckling one to the other, since they were both too short but together long enough.

"Hang in there, Dad. It's gonna be all right. Talk to me, okay? Keep talking to me." Wasn't that better than letting him drift off to sleep? What if he slept and never woke up? Yes, he'd have to keep him talking.

Linc hooked the rifle straps together and put them around his chest. He grabbed each strap to add more leverage. Straining into the straps, Linc pulled, bracing his feet as he did. "Don't worry, Dad. Breathe deep, okay? Just leave the rest to me. Remember when you were playing football, Dad? And y'all won a game? Mom said you'd put me on your shoulders and ride me around the stadium. Remember that?"

Chan smiled, or maybe he grimaced from pain. Linc couldn't be sure. "Tell me about the game where you ran ninety-five yards to make a touchdown, Dad."

It had to work. Linc strained harder. His stomach muscles, calves, and thighs felt as if they'd rip apart.

"Green Bay." Chan moaned. "Thirteen to seven. Oh."

The sling budged, just a little at first, then a bit more.

"C'mon, Dad. Thirteen to seven. The last forty-five seconds of the fourth quarter, right?" He'd heard it so many times he knew it by heart. "They'd tried to kick off sides, right?"

Chan babbled on. Linc tugged. Pulling him was hard, but it was going to work. He was glad of those secret workouts now. Chan was heavy, but he'd make it.

But where should he go? If he went the wrong way, deeper into the restricted area, it might mean his father's life. And it would be his fault. He had to find the way.

16

LINC scanned the ground as he tugged at the sling, trying to pull Chan along. If he failed to spot one of the cyanide guns, he could kill them both. He looked at the sky again. Was he going in the right direction? There was still no hint of sun.

He had to think. Their leased land was fenced. Maybe that meant that each section of land was fenced. He would simply move in one direction until he located a fence, then follow it. Or if he ran across the stream, he could follow that. But what if he were following it in the wrong direction, farther and farther away?

Chan gasped and moaned.

"Breathe deeply, Dad," Linc instructed. "In, out. Deep breaths. You're going to be okay. Great game, Dad. They gave you the game ball, didn't they?"

He might be near their lease and follow the fence the wrong way, he was so turned around. If he did, it would take him a lot longer to get back. And time was his dad's enemy; he needed a doctor.

"Gave it to the Brawn," Chan said. "The Brawn's ball, not mine."

113

Linc glanced back at his father. Was he getting delirious? "No, Dad. Your game ball. Remember?" Linc's arms and chest ached terribly. He'd never felt so much pain. But he had to keep moving, keep pulling Chan.

"No," Chan said. "All of it for Brawn. But he was never satisfied. Never. Always more. Wanted more."

That odd-shaped bush looked familiar, too familiar. Had he been traveling in a circle? Was he losing valuable time?

Linc decided he had to mark his trail somehow, let himself know he'd been there. If he could look forward and see no snapped twigs, that would help, right?

Chan moaned. "Couldn't be as good as the Brawn. He was the best."

Linc reached out and twisted a small limb, bending it in the direction he was going. "You, too, Dad. You were the best. If it hadn't been for your injuries—"

"No," Chan said. "Would've been cut. Small fish. Just small fish. Big pond. Not like Glory. Glory's little pond."

Cut? Chan wouldn't have made the pros, anyway? Twenty minutes, maybe thirty had passed. No! He was facing one of his own twig markers. He'd been going in circles again.

It was dodging those guns, going a long way around them that was throwing him off. But if he could look ahead of him and see no marked trail, and look behind him and see them, he'd know he was all right. That was it.

"You'd have made it, all right, Dad," Linc said as he struggled against the heavy load. "If I hadn't come along, you'd have made it."

The way was tedious and each breath felt as if it would explode his lungs. He was sweating, yet he was cold, so cold.

"No," Chan said. "You were a good thing in our lives. Like a second chance."

That was where they were wrong. He was nobody's second chance. He was his own only chance. He'd have to convince Chan of that when they got out of there. If they got out of there.

Then Linc spotted a fence. But which way should he go from there? He couldn't think anymore. He needed help.

What was that sound? A motor. Somewhere out there, there was a vehicle. A jeep? A pickup?

"Help!"

Linc suddenly noticed cows, hundreds of cows on the other side of the fence. Everywhere, cows. But cows couldn't help.

The cows were moving about, getting louder. That other noise was getting closer. It was definitely a motor. Motors meant people. People meant help.

Then Linc saw it, a pickup with a flatbed trailer behind it. One man was driving, and two behind him were shoving bales of hay off the trailer.

"Help!"

Linc loosened himself from the grip on the sling pulls and waved his arms. They were close, but they didn't see him. They weren't looking his way.

"Help!"

He saw a stone. If he could just throw it. Of course he could. Hadn't Chan taught him to throw a ball?

"You can't hit the side of a barn," Chan had said disgustedly.

Well, maybe he could hit something else.

Linc picked up a baseball-sized stone and drew back. His muscles tightened in rebellion. But he threw with all his might, aiming between the two men tossing bales. He missed them by a country mile, but he hit the side of the pickup.

The truck came to an immediate halt and was surrounded by cows. The driver shoved the door open, looking at his tires. He probably thought it had been a blowout.

"Help!" Linc cried, waving his arms and leaping up and down. "Help!"

He saw one, then another, finally all three men staring at him. Then they leaped from the truck and pushed through the cows, coming toward him.

As soon as they spotted Chan, one of the men stepped on the lower barbed wire and pulled up on the next. The other two stepped through and gingerly hoisted Chan up, waist high, and eased him through the fence. Numbly, Linc stepped through.

"Shot?" one man asked as the other two moved through the cows with Chan, heading toward the pickup.

"Heart," Linc said. His breath came hard and heavy. "Doctor, please. An ambulance."

"No ambulances," the driver said. "No time. We're a long way. Get in."

"Hold on, Dad." He couldn't lose him. Not just when they were finding each other.

"Hank and Sam's got him. Get in!"

The man's sharp voice shocked Linc into action. He climbed into the pickup cab.

Linc and the man, Jim Burke, introduced themselves hastily as the pickup rumbled across the bumpy terrain toward a house in the distance. When they got there, the two men leaped from the truck and unhitched the trailer.

"Hank, stay with the man. Sam, call ahead. Tell 'em we'll be on our way. Tell 'em they'd be wise to meet us halfway with an ambulance, okay?"

Linc looked back through the cab window at his father. He looked pale, and he was muttering.

The pickup bucked and bumped along the blacktop farm road while Linc stared numbly out the window at the miles of mesquite and brush.

"That was a darn good throw back there, by the way," Jim told Linc. "You go out for sports?"

Smiling slightly, Linc stared out the side window. "Not really, but I used to work out with my dad. He was a real pro."

A siren caught his attention as the pickup pulled abruptly to the shoulder of the road and Jim lowered his window, waving. The ambulance did a U-turn on the road and pulled up alongside.

Linc leaped from the cab and stood peering into the flatbed at his father. A couple of men in white, carrying a gurney with a large black bag on top, jumped from the back of the ambulance and into the flatbed.

One of the men slapped a blood-pressure band on Chan's arm and pumped the syringe. "Can you tell me your name? Age? Do you know who I am? How many fingers do you see?" He popped one question after another at Chan, who tossed his head and mumbled.

The man muttered something to his partner, who inserted a needle into Chan's other arm and began administering an IV. Obviously satisfied, they lifted Chan onto the gurney and carried him to the ambulance.

Linc followed close behind. He turned toward the two ranchers. "Thanks. Thanks a lot."

"Good luck," they said, almost in unison, as Linc crawled into the ambulance, too.

By the time Linc was settled on the bench in back, one of the men was taking blood from Chan and retaking his blood pressure. "You his son?"

"Yeah."

"Don't worry. He's going to be all right."

"Yeah?"

When Linc awoke, he blinked against the bright whiteness around him. He had to sleep. No, he had to get Chan some help. He noticed a strange smell of detergent and alcohol. Linc fluttered his lids until the blur began to come into focus. He saw dark hair. "Ginger?" His arm felt funny, heavy.

"Try not to move your arm much. There's an IV in it." A woman in a white smock smiled at him. She placed a stethoscope on his chest. It felt ice cold.

"Sorry. I'm Dr. Richards, and you're in Desertview Hospital. Can you tell me your name? Do you remember why you're here?"

"Dad! Where's my dad? But why am *I* in bed?"

"Your father's in the next bed, muttering your praises whenever he rouses. He's going to be all right. And so are you. But you're suffering from exposure. Running around in nothing but an undershirt will do that."

Linc strained to sit up and look at Chan. The doctor helped him lean forward. "Your dad's attack was not a major one," Dr. Richards said. "X rays show that he may need a bypass but not as an emergency. It's practically routine in the Houston Medical Center near your home. If he eats properly and exercises, he should regain his health."

"Mom, I need to tell my mom. She'll be worried."

"I've notified Mrs. Chandler, and they're on the way."

Linc tried to stay awake, but the blurriness was coming back. "He's all right? You're sure?"

"He's just sleeping. It's the drugs. You should sleep, too."

Linc leaned back against the stiffly starched pillowcase, smiling to himself. So Chan was muttering his praises, was he? Well, he didn't need it any more—but he'd enjoy it, all the same.